STAGE L

To Emileab

ORCHARD BOOKS
96 Leonard Street, London EC2A 4RH
Orchard Books Australia
14 Mars Road, Lane Cove, NSW 2066
ISBN 1 86039 644 5
First published in Great Britain in 1998
Paperback original
Text © Sharon Siamon 1998
The right of Shari Siamon to be identified as the author of this work has been
asserted by her in accordance with the
Copyright, Designs and Patents Act, 1988.
A CIP catalogue record for this book is available
from the British Library.
Printed in Great Britain

STAGE SCH★★L

3

★ Jenna ★
Dancing Dreams

by Geena Dare

 ORCHARD BOOKS

☆CHAPTER ONE☆

Dance Partners

Jenna waited for her turn to go spinning across the long, bare dance studio floor. Every muscle was ready. Every bit of her body was tuned to the music of the grand piano at one end of the studio.

Suddenly a burst of laughter echoed around the large empty room. The piano music crashed to a halt.

"Matt!" called Miss Adaman, the dance teacher. "Save your socialising for later!"

Jenna's concentration was shattered. She glared across the room at tall, dark-haired Matt Caruso. As usual, he was surrounded by a group of laughing girls, the centre of attention, loving every minute of it.

"Is it my turn?" Matt called. "You want me to show the rest of them how it's done?"

I could strangle him, Jenna thought furiously. He's so conceited! It's not his turn.

But Matt had already launched into his spin, the music soared from the piano again, and Jenna caught her breath.

There was something so light and magic in

Matt's dancing that he took your heart with him on his wild whirl across the wooden floor.

He came to a stop staring straight into Jenna's eyes. He was the only student in the class, boy or girl, who was her own height.

"Well?" he asked.

"Your spin was all wrong..." Jenna said. "Your arms were in the wrong position, your torso wobbled, and your feet!" Matt made her feel prickly, off balance. She wanted to wipe that smug grin off his face!

"All right, Jenna, it's your turn," Miss Adaman called.

Jenna took another deep breath. How could she concentrate now?

"Watch those arms," Matt teased. "Keep your spine straight!"

Jenna struggled to find her balance as the music began. She found herself gritting her teeth as she spun across the floor. She wanted so badly to do it right.

"That was technically perfect," Miss Adaman told her when she reached the other side of the room. "But try to put some feeling, some joy in it."

"Like Matt?" Jenna heard herself ask.

"Well, a little more like Matt wouldn't hurt." Miss Adaman glanced down at the clipboard in her hand. "As a matter of fact I'm thinking of pairing you and Matt for the dance competition."

"No, Miss Adaman, you can't!" Jenna burst out. "I can't dance with Matt." He always ruined her concentration. He did it on purpose, she was sure.

The competition next month was so important. Her whole career hung on whether she won or not. And there was no chance of winning with Matt for a partner. It was bad enough Matt had followed her from summer dance school to William S. Holly Stage School. It was bad enough they were in the same class. They couldn't be partners!

"He could be a fine young dancer with a little work," Miss Adaman said. "You can help him, Jenna."

"You don't understand," Jenna begged Miss Adaman. "He won't work on our dance – he'll ruin it for me!"

"Besides, he's the only boy in the class who comes close to you in height. You'll look good together."

Jenna turned away and gripped the barre so hard her knuckles hurt. She stared at herself in the mirror-covered wall, trying to keep back tears of anger. Why did she have to be so tall? Her reflection, a heart-shaped brown face with high cheekbones and dark eyes, stared back at her.

From the end of the room she could hear Matt's loud, irritating laugh. "Hah! You want me to be Jenna's dance partner?"

Miss Adaman's voice was low, but even from here Jenna could hear the authority in it.

"All right," Matt said. "But it won't work. You'll see." He ran across the floor and skidded to a stop in front of Jenna. "What do you think about us being partners?"

"It's hopeless. I'd rather dance with a tarantula!"

Jenna turned away angrily.

Miss Adaman watched her march out of the studio and shook her head. She worried about Jenna. That girl's a perfectionist, the same as I was at her age, she thought. If I can't get her to loosen up, she'll injure herself, just like I did! Miss Adaman's promising career had been cut short at nineteen by a torn knee ligament.

As Jenna headed down the hall towards the stairs, Matt and his friends brushed past her. They were laughing and doing little dance steps around the kids in their way, moving together like one body.

Jenna shrugged. She could never be part of a group like that – join in those stupid conversations about the latest band, or TV show or rock video. Her whole life was dancing.

When she was six, Jenna's grandmother had taken her to see her first ballet. She remembered leaning so far over the balcony that her grandmother had grabbed the back of her T-shirt to keep her from falling. Jenna had never seen anything as perfect as the world-famous ballerina, on her toes, spinning in the centre of the stage. Since that moment, nothing had mattered to her except dancing.

Her mother and sister didn't understand how much she wanted to be a great ballerina. They were always after her. "Do something important with your life," her mother would say. "Don't waste your time on that ballet stuff!" her sister Joyce would nag.

They didn't understand her dream, or why she spent hours and hours practising every day. But Jenna knew she couldn't just dream about being a great dancer. She had to work hard and have discipline. That's what Matt would never have. He had so much talent but he never practised…

There she was thinking about him again! She shrugged her dance equipment bag on to the other shoulder. Forget Matt! Jenna shoved the thought of Matt's laughing eyes aside and hurried down the stairs to the canteen.

With any luck, her best friends Abbi and Lauren would be there. They would understand.

☆CHAPTER TWO☆

Warrior Princess

The canteen at William S. Holly was a huge open space on the first floor. At lunch time it was mobbed. 'Holly' as the kids called it, was an old and famous stage school. Many of its students had gone on to become stars in the performing arts.

Jenna threaded her way through groups of singers, dancers and actors to the special table their group had staked out during auditions last summer.

Five of them had auditioned together. Jenna and Matt, for the dance programme, Lauren Graham, for vocal music, and Dan Reeve and Abbi Reilly, for drama.

"Hi, Jen!" Abbi waved her over. "Wait till you hear this!" Jenna grinned. You just had to take one look at Abbi to see that someday, she would be a sensation in films or television. She had already starred in a production of *Dracula*, even though this was her first year at Stage School.

"What's up?" Jenna asked. She liked Abbi, even though with her outgoing personality, flying gold-blonde curls, and bright blue eyes, Abbi was her complete opposite in almost every way.

"My dad wants me to come to Australia to visit him this Christmas." Abbi's eyes were dancing. "I haven't seen him since I was a little kid. And I'm dying to see Australia!"

"Is that why you're jumping up and down like a kangaroo?" Jenna asked, smiling again. "What's wrong, Jenna?" Lauren was sitting quietly at the end of the table. Her smooth short hair was parted in the middle and tucked behind her ears. She had soft grey eyes and pale skin.

"Trust you to notice something's bothering me," Jenna collapsed beside her with a grateful sigh. Calm, sensitive Lauren was in many ways her best friend.

"I'm sorry, Jenna," Abbi said. "It's just that I'm so excited about Australia. Dad said I could come for the whole holiday. Just imagine, it will be summer down there and the beaches…" Abbi threw out her arms.

"Wait!" Lauren held up her hand. "Let's hear what happened to Jenna."

"It's Matt," Jenna groaned.

"What happened?" Lauren looked alarmed. She felt her face getting hot. She tried to hide her feelings about Matt from the others.

"Nothing…but Miss Adaman made us partners for the dance competition. I can't dance with him…"

"Why not?" Abbi asked eagerly. "You two would look great together."

"I just can't…" Jenna shook her head. "Matt

never takes dancing seriously."

"Did I hear my name spoken of with disdain?" Matt bounded up behind her with their friend Dan in tow. "You're too serious, Jenna James. If your toes aren't bleeding you feel like you're not working hard enough!"

"What's all this about?" Dan asked. He was as odd-looking as Matt was tall, dark and handsome. His ears stuck out, and his mouth was too large. It was only when Dan was on stage that his real personality came out. He was a brilliant comic actor.

"There's a competition for all the dance students in the school," Jenna explained. "We have to create a dance with a partner, and perform it in front of judges. The two winners get a scholarship to a dance seminar in New York during the spring break. It's for two weeks."

"Two weeks!" Matt said. "I can't go to New York for two weeks! I have to work in my family's store, and make lots of money!" He rubbed his fingers together.

"See!" Jenna threw out her graceful arms. "He doesn't even want to win. This scholarship could be important for our entire career."

"You and your precious career!" Matt snorted. "We're only thirteen. We've got lots of time."

"Dancers have to start young. I want to be a working dancer by the time I'm sixteen," Jenna said. "That's only three years. If you don't care about a dance career, what are you doing here?"

"Enjoying Lauren's company," Matt threw his

arm around Lauren's shoulders. "She never gives me a hard time."

Lauren flushed bright pink. She both loved and hated the way Matt treated her like a little sister. And she wished Jenna wouldn't be so hard on Matt. She knew that deep down, it hurt him.

"I wouldn't give you a hard time if you'd only try," Jenna told Matt. "You're just throwing away your talent."

"So?" Matt glared at her.

"I think it sounds exciting!" Abbi told Matt. "Even if you can't go to New York, you can help Jenna win the scholarship."

"He never will," Jenna glared at him. "He doesn't know how to fight for something he wants."

"Listen to the Warrior Princess!" Matt cried. "To you, the whole world is a battle that you have to win. Well, I'm as sorry as you are that we have to be partners. Come on, Dan. Let's go."

"Never mind, I'm leaving." Jenna turned away, stung by Matt's harsh words.

"Want to come to my house after school?" Abbi called after her. "Lauren and I are going to make fudge and watch soaps."

"I can't," Jenna called over her shoulder. "I have to practise." She marched with a straight back and head held high, towards the canteen doors.

"This is not going to be a fun-filled few weeks," Matt said. "I know that walk. She's really mad."

Lauren saw a certain look flicker across Matt's face as he watched Jenna disappear through the doors. She spent hours studying Matt's face, and she'd seen that look before. He pretends not to care, but he does, she thought. And no wonder – Jenna looks like a princess. So tall and proud and beautiful.

☆CHAPTER THREE☆

Home Hassles

Jenna ran lightly down the wide steps of William S. Holly after school. It was a cool bright October afternoon. The sun was just going down, and its slanting rays blinded Jenna for a moment. She almost bumped into a tall young man in a black leather jacket standing at the bottom of the steps.

He gave Jenna a quick glance and she murmured an apology. Good-looking, in a weird kind of way, Jenna thought. He was probably waiting for one of the senior students. She forgot the strange young man on her long bus ride home. Her small, two-storey brick house was on a tree-lined street near the university. It was old, but Jenna loved it. They had lived here ever since coming from Grenada, when she was a baby. Her father had died shortly after they arrived, and Jenna had been brought up by her mum and her older sister Joyce.

She could see Joyce in the kitchen at the back of the house as she came though the front door.

"Dinner in ten minutes!" Joyce was banging pots on the stove. She was tall, like Jenna, eight years older and an engineering student at the university. She wore her curly black hair cut close to her head, gold earrings and bright shirts with African motifs.

"How was school?" she asked as Jenna paused in the kitchen doorway. There were pencil marks on the door frame where she measured her height as she grew.

"Horrible. I have Matt Caruso as a dancing partner for the scholarship competition." Jenna held her hand flat on top of her head, then spun around to see where her finger touched the door frame. It seemed a bit higher than the mark she made last month. "Help!" she said. "I'm still growing!"

"Of course you're growing. You're only thirteen." Joyce was cooking something that smelled delicious.

"But I'm going to be nearly two metres tall," Jenna moaned.

"So?"

"Ballerinas can't be that tall."

"Then why do you want to dance that old ballet stuff. All those prissy little white costumes…"

"Stop that!" Jenna said. "How would you feel if someone said engineering was only for guys? Ballet costumes are not all white, and neither are the dancers, if that's what you're trying to say."

"OK!" Joyce held up her hand. "I'm just trying to help. Let's not get into a fight before dinner."

Jenna took the lid off a pot and sniffed the great smell. "I'll just have a bit of that," she said.

"Come on, you have to eat," Joyce scolded. "It's

not going to make you shorter if you miss dinner."

"No, but I still want to work on my dance for a couple of hours," Jenna shook her head. "I don't want my stomach weighed down with food."

Joyce gave her a hard look. "You have to watch you don't get sick," she said. "I can't remember the last time I saw you eat a good meal."

☆

After dinner there was a knock at Jenna's front door. She opened it to find Lauren on the front porch.

"Hi, Jenna," she said. "I'm sorry I didn't call, but as soon as I got back from Abbi's I had a chance to ride downtown with my dad. He's going to the opera, but I just jumped out and said I had to borrow a book from you."

"Your dad must have loved that!" Jenna hated to interrupt her dance practice but she felt sorry for Lauren. Her parents had their hearts set on her becoming an opera singer.

"He knows I don't like opera," Lauren said, "but he never gives up trying."

They chatted about parents while Jenna got her a drink and some cookies from the kitchen.

"Aren't you having any?" Lauren asked as they headed upstairs.

"Oh, no," Jenna waved a slim hand. "I can't touch that stuff."

Lauren sighed. "You're so dedicated," she said. "I could never give up junk food for singing."

Once they were comfortably settled in Jenna's upstairs bedroom, Lauren looked up from her

☆**17**☆

drink, her grey eyes serious. "I really want to talk about Matt," she said.

"I don't." Jenna was sitting cross-legged on the end of her bed, hugging her favourite pillow.

"No, wait! After you had that fight in the canteen, Matt got this look on his face, as if you really hurt him."

"Hah!" Jenna leapt up, almost hitting her head on the ceiling. "Hurt looks are easy. Hours and hours of practising are hard. You should see Matt in dance class. All he does is clown around." Jenna made another long-legged leap to the floor.

"Does he?" Lauren asked, wistfully. "He must be funny to watch."

"It's not funny," Jenna said. "He even makes Miss Adaman laugh. It brings down the whole tone of the class."

She glanced at Lauren who was leaning back against the pillows at the foot of the bed. Her eyes were dreamy.

"You still like him, don't you?" Jenna said gently. "I thought you'd got over that."

"I guess I haven't," Lauren sighed. "Every time I look at him, my knees turn to water. I can't stop thinking about him…"

"Then I feel sorry for you," Jenna folded her long legs under her once again and perched on the round rug at Lauren's feet, "because the only person Matt Caruso loves is himself!"

"I'll talk to him about the dance competition," Lauren promised. "Sometimes he listens to me."

☆

Jenna's mother was coming in from a late shift at her library job just as Lauren was leaving.

"It's good to see you having friends over," Mrs James smiled. "Is Lauren in your dance class?"

"No, she's a singer," Jenna shook her head. "She was in my audition group this summer."

"I'd like to meet more of your friends." Jenna's mother hung up her coat on a hook in the hall.

"Meaning?" Jenna stood poised on the stairs, looking down at her mother.

"Meaning, it's nice to see you're starting to have a normal life. Friends outside your dance class."

Jenna swallowed the words that wanted to spill out. This was an old, old argument with her mother. Have a life. Be more like normal teenagers. Don't miss your growing up years.

Nobody, Jenna thought, as she fled back up the stairs, nobody understood that dancing was all she wanted – being the best dancer in the world, that's all she dreamed of. Not boys, not friends, not clothes, not anything else!

☆

In her own small bedroom, Abbi gazed happily at all the pictures of Australia she had tacked on to the walls. There were koala bears and kangaroos, bright-coloured parrots and long, golden beaches.

"I'm going to see all this," Abbi hugged herself with joy. Two more months…"

At that moment, her nine-year-old brother Joe came bursting into the room. "Is it true you're going to see Dad?" he blurted. "Why can't I come?"

Joe had red hair that stuck out in spikes. Right

now, his face was even redder than his hair.

"He only has the money for one ticket," Abbi said. "You can go when you're older." Abbi's father had left when she was ten and she missed him terribly. He understood her wild extremes, her need for adventure, much better than her sensible, organised mother did. Until she started at William S. Holly, Abbi thought she would never fit in with any group.

Joe was fooling around with a photo of himself, Dad and Abbi on Abbi's dresser. "Sometimes I can't even remember what Dad looks like."

"Leave that alone, you'll drop it." Abbi grabbed the picture.

"Why can't I have it – he's my dad, too."

"Maybe Mum can get you a copy, but this one's mine." Abbi hugged the photo in its silver frame. "Why don't you start writing to Dad, like I do?" She had been writing to him, every week, even though he hardly ever wrote back. She had earned this trip!

"Oh, forget it, I can't write very well, anyway." Joe shrugged and ran out of the room. A few seconds later, Abbi heard his video game blaring from the TV in his room.

I'll talk to Dad about Joe when I'm in Australia, Abbi thought. I'll get him to send a new picture. Joe was doing badly in school and was always in trouble. Video games were his escape from the real world.

☆CHAPTER FOUR☆

We All Fall Down

"Matt, try again!" Miss Adaman's voice came ringing across the studio's expanse of wooden floor.

Jenna and Matt had been practising lifts for what felt like an hour. The rest of the students, bored and restless, stood and sat around the edge of the studio space, watching.

The autumn sun, beating in through the windows on one side of the room, made it feel hot and stuffy.

Matt had broken into a sweat.

"You have to make it look like she floats upwards, and hold her without effort," Miss Adaman called. "Try once more."

"If only you weren't such a horse," Matt teased, as he lifted Jenna again.

"I thought you had such great muscles from heaving all those boxes of fruit around at the store," she whispered back.

"Stop!" Miss Adaman finally called. "We can see the strain," she told Matt. "It spoils the effect if you look like you're lifting a dumb-bell at a weight-lifting class."

There were small ripples of laughter from the other students.

"That wasn't meant as a joke," Miss Adaman warned. "All right, once more…"

The music began again. Jenna took a few light steps and leapt. She felt herself sliding through Matt's arms and landed awkwardly on one knee.

"Uh-oh, I dropped the dumb-bell," Matt said.

There were titters around the room. No one liked to laugh when a dancer fell, but Matt was such a clown!

Jenna picked herself up as Miss Adaman hurried over. "Are you all right?" she asked anxiously.

"Maybe just a bruised knee," Jenna winced as she stood up, "that's all."

"Matt, this isn't funny!" Miss Adaman said, turning to him.

"You can see it isn't going to work – the two of us being partners," Jenna told her. "He isn't strong enough…"

"I'm strong enough to lift a normal human being," Matt said. "Not a giraffe!"

"I'll talk to both of you after class," said Miss Adaman and motioned to the pianist to begin again.

At the end of their class Jenna and Matt joined their teacher at the piano.

"I've got science." Matt glanced at his watch.

"Just let me work with someone else," Jenna begged her.

"You'll both stay and listen to this," Miss Adaman said. "Jenna, in your career, you're going to have to dance with partners you don't like. Part of being professional is learning not to let your feelings get in the way of your performance."

Jenna was silent, choking back her anger.

"Matt," Miss Adaman went on, "lifts aren't just about strength. Balance is involved, and timing. I'd like to send you both to a special Saturday workshop at the Young People's Dance Theatre. My friend Jared Wesker teaches it. He can help you."

"The YPDT?" Jenna breathed. "It's famous."

"I work on Saturdays," Matt said.

Miss Adaman raised her eyebrows. "Aren't you a little young to have a job?"

"It's my mum and dad's store. Caruso's Fruit and Vegetables," Matt said proudly. "I've been helping out on the weekends since I was nine years old."

"Ah," Miss Adaman said. "I see. Well, talk it over with your parents. Maybe they could spare you for a few weekends. I'll call them, if you like."

"No, it's OK, I'll ask them," he said.

Miss Adaman gathered her clipboard and notes. "Let me know as soon as you can," she told him. "I'll need to make arrangements with Jared. Now, you'd better run to your science class."

Jenna gathered her books and gear and ran down the shiny studio floor after him.

"Matt, please," she begged. "Young People's Dance Theatre–"

"Forget it," he shrugged.

"You're not even going to ask your parents, are you?"

Their argument spilled out into the hallway. With the change of classes the hall was full of hurrying, noisy kids. Jenna almost had to shout to make Matt hear.

"Couldn't you just stop working on Saturdays until–"

Matt wheeled round. "Saturdays are for having fun, making some money." He strode away from her.

Jenna ran to catch up. "Just one Saturday? Couldn't you give the workshop a chance?"

Matt stopped again. "What for? I'm never going to dance well enough to satisfy you, so what's the use?"

"Couldn't you just try?" Jenna could feel her face getting hot. She hated to beg, but the workshop was her last chance. "What do you need money for, anyway?"

Matt stopped and stared at her. "For fun! You've heard of fun, haven't you? Having a good time, enjoying yourself?"

He was teasing again, but Jenna ignored it. "Please, for me? I want to win this scholarship and I need your help." She felt amazed as the words came out of her mouth.

Matt's face was a mask of surprise. "So, you're asking me, one human being to another, to come to this workshop with you?"

"Yes, I'm asking you, I'm begging you – this Saturday?" Jenna stammered.

"All right, I'll think about it," Matt promised. "Oh, hi, Lauren," he said over her shoulder.

Jenna spun round. Lauren was behind her, her grey eyes huge in her pale face. "Hi," she said in a strangled voice, and then brushed past them.

"What's wrong with her?" Matt said, peering through the mass of bodies swarming after her.

I know what's wrong, Jenna thought. She thinks I just made a date with Matt for Saturday. She must feel so hurt, after she told me how she feels. I'll have to explain…with me it's just dancing, nothing else!

☆CHAPTER FIVE☆

Lauren's Song

Lauren ran down the hall toward the music room, leaving Jenna and Matt behind. Her heart felt like it was breaking. "What an idiot I am," she muttered. "I've been talking to Jenna about Matt, and promising to talk to Matt about Jenna when they're both–"

She swallowed a lump in her throat – when they're both working it out just fine without me.

"What am I doing at Stage School?" Lauren asked herself for the zillionth time. "Why don't I just leave?"

She had never meant to attend Stage School. She'd come to the William S. Holly auditions just to help her friend, Martha. But when Martha didn't get in and Lauren did, Matt was the one who'd persuaded her to stay.

"Hey, Lauren...wait for me!" It was Matt. He came racing down the hall, blocking her path. "I promised Mrs Schumacher I'd help move the stuff in the music room today."

"Oh...what stuff?" Lauren felt all her anger dissolve as she looked up at his smiling face. She was here, at 'Holly' just so she could be close to Matt. It wasn't smart, but she couldn't help it.

Matt was staring at her, puzzled. "Aren't you having some kind of special performance today? Mrs Schumacher said she needed some help rearranging the room."

"I remember," Lauren said. "It's a Celtic music group." It could be music from outer space and it wouldn't matter to her, she thought, as long as Matt was there.

The two of them had reached the music room, and inside, students were already shoving back the chairs to enlarge the small stage at the front. Their chatter and excitement was amplified by the excellent acoustics.

Lauren felt herself outside all of it as she watched Matt showing off. He balanced a chair on one leg, then piled six chairs and lifted them like they weighed nothing.

The piercing sound of a tin whistle, and drums, brought Lauren back to her senses. The Celtic group swirled down the centre aisle. They gathered the music students around them, and invited them to join in. Lauren noticed that Matt had stayed to listen.

There were three young men and three women in the group called the Lilith Singers. They were dressed in medieval costumes, and played antique instruments like the Celtic harp.

"We're going to teach you a very old song," the pipe player announced. He reminded Lauren of an older Matt. He was tall, with tightly curled hair, and a small beard. "Does anyone know 'Green Grow the Rushes-O'?"

The music began, and Lauren found herself enjoying the singing. This music suited her light soprano voice, her perfect pitch. The leader indicated that she should sing a verse by herself.

> *I'll sing you three-O*
> *Green grow the rushes-O*
> *What is your three-O?*
> *Three, three, the rivals...*

There was something old and magical in this music. It swept Lauren out of herself. For a moment she forgot all about Matt, her shyness and all her problems.

At the back of the room, Matt stood, startled by Lauren's voice. She sounded like a completely different person from the quiet little Lauren they all knew. He was sorry when the others joined in with the chorus.

At the end, he ran down to the stage to congratulate her.

The group's piper, whose name was William, had already cornered Lauren. "You should come to the Medieval Fair in High Park a week from Sunday," William said. "There'll be lots of groups. You might enjoy it."

"Thank you," Lauren's grey eyes were shining. "I'd love to come."

"That was pretty good singing," Matt said as they went back out into the hall.

"The songs are so much better than some of

those big show tunes that Mr O'Brien is always trying to get us to sing at the top of our lungs," Lauren laughed. "I guess I'm just not a Broadway belter."

"No," Matt gave her a friendly hug. "But I like listening to you sing. Do you think you'll go to that fair?"

"I might." Lauren's heart felt like a yo-yo on a string. One minute it rattled around the soles of her feet, the next it was zinging somewhere around her ears. Matt liked her singing! Maybe next he'd notice the person connected to the voice.

"I'd like to come, too, but I have to work on Saturdays."

Lauren looked up in astonishment. "Aren't you going somewhere with Jenna?"

"Oh, yeah, I forgot!" Matt made a face. "Jenna's twisting my arm to go to a dance workshop for this competition thing."

Lauren's heart felt like it would burst with relief and joy. "You should go," she told Matt. "The dance competition is more important than this fair."

"Do you think so?" Matt asked her. "Well, I might. But I'll do it because you said so, not Jenna."

☆

"Everybody should go to that Medieval Fair and give Lauren some support," Matt told Abbi and Dan. He found them with Jenna at their usual table in the canteen. "I heard her sing just now. She was amazing!"

Abbi looked up from a script she was trying to

memorise for acting class. "When is it?" she said. "I have to baby-sit for my brother after school."

"It's on Saturday," Matt explained. "I'd go, but I'm being dragged off to some dance class." He glowered at Jenna.

Jenna felt her heart bounce. Matt was going to come to the Young People's Dance Theatre! They could work on their dance for the competition. She was sure Matt would love getting instruction from the famous Jared Wesker!

"I think it's a great idea to go to the fair," said Dan. "Abbi could wear a long gown, and how would I look in a fool's cap, with bells?" He made a comic face. Dan looked hopefully at Abbi. It was clear to everyone that he'd go anywhere to spend a day with her.

"I can't," Abbi sighed. "Saturday's my mum's busiest day – she's doing this big property deal. I'll be looking after dear old Joe again."

"You could bring him to the fair," Dan suggested.

"Oh, he'd love that," Abbi laughed. "Joe the vid-kid at a medieval fair. He'd be bored in five minutes. And when he's bored, he's dangerous."

"Come on, bring him," Dan urged. "I can handle your little brother."

"It's going to be so great to go off to Australia and leave him behind," Abbi sighed. "He's driving me crazy these days."

"Come on, Abbi, we've got to support Lauren," Matt urged. "Maybe they'll get her to sing in public."

Jenna watched Matt's eager face. Lauren would love to hear this, she thought. Matt would really like to be listening to her sing, instead of dancing with me. She wriggled uncomfortably, as though something had just grabbed her insides and given them a wicked twist.

The twisted feeling stayed with Jenna as she got her stuff from her locker and made her way out into the autumn afternoon. Lauren was her best friend. She should be happy that Matt had finally noticed her...so why did she feel so miserable?

The same tall guy in the black jacket was standing near the entrance to the school. He stared quite openly at the kids running down the steps – as though he was looking for someone. I'll have to ask the others if they've noticed him, Jenna thought, as she ran to the corner to catch her bus.

☆CHAPTER SIX☆

Matt Gets Mad

Matt and Jenna took the bus downtown to the Young People's Dance Theatre on Saturday. Jenna found her heart pounding excitedly, just being in the theatrical district. This was where all the famous ballet companies came to perform!

Beside her, Matt was still talking about Lauren. "She's so different from the rest of us," he said. "There's none of this 'I'm the world's greatest singer' stuff with Lauren."

"She's the best," Jenna agreed. She knew she should feel glad for Lauren – Matt really liked her. But instead she felt something else, that same nasty twist in her insides.

"I mean, I've always thought of Lauren as just a kid, like my little sister, but when she sings, she sounds…" Matt shrugged, at a loss for words.

"You've just discovered Lauren is a real person," Jenna said. "Congratulations, Matt."

"You know, you are impossible to talk to," Matt flushed angrily. He stood up suddenly and bent down to peer out the window. "Come on, I think we went past our stop."

☆

Jared Wesker, the head of the Young People's Dance Theatre was short and slim, with a mane of silver grey hair and long sideburns.

"My friend Mary Adaman said you'd be coming," Mr Wesker welcomed them. "Just stand over there and watch while we go through some notes on our last performance." He waved them to a spot near the wall.

The Dance Theatre dancers were all in their twenties. Jenna forgot Lauren, and Matt. She drew in her breath with delight. These dancers had toured all over the world.

When they had gathered on the floor, Jared Wesker held up his hand for silence. "We have two William Holly students dancing with us this morning," he announced. "Two of their best, I presume," he nodded to Jenna and Matt with a small smile.

"What a twit," Matt muttered under his breath.

Jenna kicked him savagely in the back of the calf.

"Ouch!" Matt proclaimed. "Why did you do that?"

Jared Wesker's superior smile turned to a look of outrage. "You are not at High School now," he said. "Please try to behave like adults."

Jenna wanted to melt into a puddle of shame! How could she lose her temper like that? Mr Wesker would think they were infants! She glared at Matt and he gave her his most maddening smirk. Oh, this was not going to work!

But Matt soon settled down and joined the other dancers in the warm-up exercises. Out of the corner of her eye, Jenna could see that Jared Wesker was impressed with his energy and talent.

Then Jared paired them off to practise lifts. The other pairs soared through their exercises, turning the studio into a swirl of light and flowing movement.

Then it was their turn. Matt took his position. Jenna floated into his arms...

"Stop!" Jared Wesker thundered. "Is she a sack of potatoes? Where did you learn to lift – heaving vegetables in a farmer's market?"

OH, NO! Jenna gasped inwardly. Of all the examples to use, why did Jared Wesker have to pick heaving vegetables!

She could see an angry red flush creeping up the back of Matt's neck. He shot her a look that would scorch earth.

"Watch me," Jared sighed. "Jenna, take your position." The music began again as Jenna leaped into Jared's arms and was held aloft without so much as a tremor. It felt wonderful.

"Very good," he let her down into the final position. "This young woman knows what she's doing. Why don't you try again," Jared Wesker said to Matt.

Once more the music began.

Once more Matt tried the lift.

"She's not a box of plums, either," Jared droned in his weary voice. "Your arms need to be looser, looser!"

"That's it!" Matt put Jenna down. "I'm out of here!"

"Matt–!" Jenna begged.

"I have to...uh...get some fresh air," Matt told Mr Wesker. "It's too stuffy in here." And he glared at the teacher as he ran out, slamming the street door behind him.

Jared Wesker dismissed Matt with a wave of his hand. "If you can get a grip on yourself, come back." He turned back to his group of dancers. They moved as a flock of birds to his direction, seeming not to notice Matt's exit.

Jenna hurried after Matt. He was walking away from the building, flicking his jean jacket like a wet towel, expressing rage with his whole body. He turned a corner on to a busy street thronged with Saturday morning shoppers.

"Wait!" Jenna begged him, catching up. "Here, let me buy you a cold drink, Matt." And she pulled him into the open door of a coffee shop and held on to his sleeve so he wouldn't run off while she ordered two cans of Coke. She found a table near the window and they sat down together.

Matt glared out of the window at the people strolling by.

"Matt – I'm sorry!" Jenna began. She had to get him to go back to the workshop.

"My family's store has been feeding people in this city for three generations," Matt's brown eyes were stormy. "But that jerk is too good for vegetables. He probably never even shops for himself – sends out for food. I don't belong in that world, Jenna!"

"Yes, you do," Jenna had a sudden impulse to grab Matt's hand, but she didn't dare. "You're not the only one who feels like they don't belong. People think I'm from the Caribbean, so I must like reggae music…"

"To that guy, I'm just a meathead," Matt went on.

"Who says dancers all have to be like Jared Wesker?" said Jenna. "You've got–" she was suddenly shocked to hear herself say it, "something really special when you dance."

"It's no use trying to butter me up," Matt shook his head. "I'm not going back in there."

Jenna felt a spurt of anger. She had been sincere, and Matt thought she was just flattering him to get her way. He *was* a meathead!

"Jared Wesker might be able to teach you something, you know," she flared.

"Nothing I can't learn on my own," Matt shot back, equally angry.

We always end up like this, Jenna thought, looking down at her drink in despair.

At that moment she felt a light tap on her shoulder and looked up.

☆CHAPTER SEVEN☆

Perfect Height

Jenna's brown eyes widened in surprise. It was the man she had bumped into at the school – the guy who had been standing on the steps, watching. He was dressed in black, as usual, and carrying an enormous camera case. He held out his hand to Jenna. "I'm Norman Mars, from the Lara Lake Modelling Agency," he said.

Jenna stared up at him.

"May I sit down?" he asked her.

Jenna glanced at Matt. He shrugged, but under his attempt to look cool, Jenna could see he was watchful.

"I guess so," said Jenna.

"I'm a talent scout," Norman announced. "I look for people with model potential."

Jenna and Matt exchanged glances.

"I've been watching you, since you ran up the street," Norman folded his tall frame onto the chair and leaned his elbows on the table. "You have a great look...you're the perfect height, too."

Jenna felt embarrassed. She must have looked like an idiot chasing Matt. "I...I think I've seen you at the school," she said. "I go to William S. Holly."

"I check out all the performing arts schools," Norman nodded. "I think I have seen you there." He pulled a glossy business card out of his pocket. "How old are you?" he asked.

"Why?" Jenna asked. She felt uncomfortable giving personal information to a stranger.

"I promise you, this is on the level," Norman smiled a wide, white-toothed smile. "My job is to keep an eye out for young women of the right age, height, and look. If you're under fifteen, you've got all the rest, believe me. My agency might be interested in offering you a very good contract. You should get in touch…" He pointed to a phone number on the card.

Jenna picked it up. "I'm only thirteen," she muttered.

"That's a perfect age to get into the business." Norman Mars grinned again. "We recruit some girls when they're eleven. It's on the level," he said again. "I know a top model prospect when I see one."

"I'm not a model, I'm a dancer," said Jenna.

"A dancer? How perfect!" Norman flashed his smile. "I'd like to call your parents," Norman went on. "If you'll give me your name, and phone number."

"I'm not sure…" Jenna hesitated.

"Why not?" Matt said. "It might be interesting."

"It's just my mum," said Jenna. She wrote her number on the back of the card with Jenna James underneath it.

"Jenna James – terrific name." Norman's smile glistened. "You'll be hearing from us," he said, and he turned and walked out of the coffee shop. From the window they watched him lope across the street.

"Wow!" Matt said. "You hear about being discovered. I wonder if he'll really call your mother?" He had recovered his good mood.

"I don't care," Jenna stared at Matt. "I want to be a dancer, not a model…"

Matt ignored her. "I'm in the presence of greatness!" he said. "I mean, listen to what the man said – a great look, great potential. You could go straight to the top. I mean you're gorgeous, and you are the perfect height for a model…" His eyes twinkled mischievously. "Come on, Jenna. You can't just sit here and pretend nothing has happened!"

Jenna stood up. "Will you come back to the dance workshop with me?"

"To old Whisker Wesker? Never!" Matt said. "You couldn't get me back there if you towed me behind a truck!"

Jenna turned away.

Matt was up in a second, holding her arm. "I'm sorry, Jen, but I can't go back. Aren't you just a little bit excited about what just happened? There could be a lot of money…"

"No," Jenna pulled away. "I don't want to go strutting down a fashion show catwalk like some kind of stick figure doll. I don't care about the money – I just want to dance!"

"You really mean it, don't you?" There was a mixture of admiration and wonder in Matt's voice.

Jenna turned to look at him. His face had lost the teasing look. For a second she hardly recognised him.

"You're like Lauren," Matt went on. "This Stage School stuff means more to you than just fame and glory, doesn't it?" He stopped, and looked at his watch. "Hey! We still have time to make it to that medieval fair at High Park and maybe listen to Lauren sing."

Once more, Jenna felt the twisted ache inside. She had forgotten all about Lauren's singing, but Matt had remembered. He had wanted to go to the fair all along – he had never wanted to go with her to the dance workshop.

As they walked side by side along the busy street, Jenna glanced at his handsome profile. Her feelings about Matt were all mixed up.

"Hey!" he said suddenly. "Watch this!"

He raced ahead of her, put both hands on top of a parking meter and soared over it in one great, leapfrogging jump.

There was such joy, such freedom in that soaring leap that Jenna heard herself gasp.

Matt was halfway down the block, leapfrogging over every parking meter. People were smiling and clapping as he passed.

"Want me to show you how to do it?" He came swaggering back, his brown eyes dancing. "You're the perfect height!"

"No," Jenna shook her head. "It's too

dangerous. I could twist my ankle or tear a ligament–"

"You're hopeless," he laughed. "Loosen up a little!"

Why does Matt have to say stuff like that? Jenna thought, as she walked beside him. Everything that had seemed so clear, now felt muddled. There was Matt pulling her to one side – away from the discipline of ballet. Have fun! he seemed to say. Come on, be alive.

And now, she thought, there was this modelling thing pulling her another way. Be glamorous and famous. Make money. That's what every girl wants, right?

Jenna tossed back her braided ponytail. "Matt," she said, "why did you come to Holly? Why did you choose the dance programme?"

Matt did a quick shuffle so that they were walking in synch, right foot, then left. "At first I just did it for laughs. I took that summer course to do something different. All the guys in our neighbourhood are sports fanatics – I wanted something else. It was like a dare…" he tried to explain. "And then, when I got there – there was you!"

"Me?" Jenna was stunned. "What do you mean?"

"I'd never seen anybody like you…like some kind of fairy-tale person."

"Don't you mean a warrior princess?" Jenna said.

"Well, sometimes. But you looked so cool – and the way you danced!" Matt gave another leap in the air. "And then I started to like dancing, too, so I followed you to the Holly auditions."

"You came because of me?"

"I never really thought I'd get in," Matt explained. "But you kept pushing me, and here I am."

Jenna stared at him. Matt smiled back his most maddening grin.

"And you're still pushing me – and I'm still trying to get you to loosen up and have more fun. Hey – how about that fence post? I can show you how to do the jump. It's easy."

"No…not today. Let's go. The fair will be over before we get there." Jenna raced ahead, as if she could outrun the torrent of feelings pouring through her.

☆CHAPTER EIGHT☆

Come to the Fair!

The grass in High Park was green from the autumn rain. All the leaves had fallen from the trees that studded the six block square of city park. They made a bright carpet of orange and red and yellow that crunched under Matt's and Jenna's feet.

As they crossed the park they could hear the notes of the piper, the beating of the Celtic drum. You might have thought you were back in the medieval times, Jenna thought, except for a TV truck standing next to the curb, and the sound of traffic.

Dan, true to his plan, was dressed in a fool's hat that stuck out in points in all directions. He grinned at them when they joined the small crowd watching him juggle two brightly-coloured sticks.

"I didn't know Dan could juggle," Matt said. "He's a man of many talents, but you wouldn't catch me wearing that stupid hat."

At that moment, Abbi and Lauren came dashing up. Abbi's gold-blonde hair was flying around her face and she was trying to run in her long medieval costume.

"I've lost Joe," she gasped. "You haven't seen him, have you?"

"We just got here," Jenna explained. Poor Abbi. Her little brother Joe was getting to be more trouble all the time.

"How long has he been gone?" Matt asked, gazing around the crowd for the short, red-haired boy.

"I don't know," Abbi looked frightened. "Lauren and I were listening to the music, and I thought he was right there beside me. Then suddenly he was gone."

"We'll find him," Matt assured her. "He can't have gone very far."

"You don't know Joe," Abbi groaned. "I keep telling Mum we can't keep him cooped up in the apartment all the time. When he gets out, he just goes crazy!"

"Does your mum know you're here?" Jenna had a quick thought.

"No-o-o," Abbi admitted. "She'd never let me take Joe downtown. But I just wanted to hear Lauren sing so badly."

"It's all right," Matt said again. "Let's get Dan." He jumped up to look over the heads of the crowd and waved his arms at Dan. Dan saw him, clapped his sticks together, gave a quick bow to the applauding audience, and made his way towards them.

"What's up?"

"Joe's run away," Abbi gasped quickly. "I've got to find him…"

Quickly they fanned out across the park. Jenna teamed up with Lauren. "Poor Abbi," Lauren said. "It's a lot of responsibility looking after a nine-year-old all the time."

Jenna nodded. "We're lucky we're the youngest in our families."

Lauren suddenly stopped. "What are you and Matt doing here? What happened to the dance workshop?"

"It's a long story," Jenna made a face. "Let's find Joe, first. Then I'll tell you."

They checked the ice cream vendor's wagon, the sausage stand, and all the obvious places a nine-year-old might be. Ten minutes later, they had covered the whole park without catching a glimpse of his red hair. They met the others back at the small, makeshift stage where the Celtic musicians had stopped performing, and were standing in a group together.

"He's not here," Abbi said tearfully. "He must have left the park to look for a video arcade."

"We'll all help you look for him," said William, the group's leader. "Let's spread out and check the streets around the park."

But after twenty minutes of combing the streets around High Park, the searchers were discouraged. "It's as if he vanished into thin air!" Abbi paced up and down in her long, medieval gown. "Maybe he's completely lost!"

"Shouldn't you call your mum?" asked Jenna.

Abbi nodded miserably. "Poor Mum. It's so hard looking after Joe without Dad. He's getting wilder all the time."

All at once they heard a shout. "Over here!"

William was standing at the back of the TV crew's truck. "I think I found your brother," he said. "The New Age man, lost in his electronic world."

The equipment truck had big double doors at the back. One of them was partly open. Abbi and Dan, Jenna, Lauren and Matt peered inside. Joe, wearing huge earphones, was gazing at a portable monitor.

Abbi leaped up into the back of the truck, kicking at her heavy skirt. "WHAT ARE YOU DOING IN HERE!" she bellowed. Joe came jumping down out of the truck, still wearing the oversized headphones. He peeled them off and grinned at his rescuers.

By now the TV technicians and quite a crowd were gathering.

"They have all kinds of neat stuff in there," Joe shook his head in admiration. "Video cameras, and sound recording stuff. I've been watching you all wandering around. It looked like you were looking for something."

"We were looking for you!" Abbi stamped her foot. "Everyone in the park has been looking for you."

"Oh!" Joe shrugged. "Well, I was here, the whole time. I don't know why you're so upset."

"Well, next time," Matt ruffled his hair, "tell someone before you disappear."

"I'm sorry he wrecked the fair," Abbi

apologized to Lauren, when everything had returned to normal.

"That's all right," Lauren smiled. "That was their last set of the day. Anyway, William is teaching me some new songs, and he wants me to perform with the group a week from tomorrow. They're doing a concert at the Roxy."

"That's great!" Abbi exclaimed.

"He asked Dan to help out with the concert," Lauren went on, "and there might be jobs for all of us backstage."

They were all walking across the park to the bus stop. Lauren and Matt were together, with Jenna and Dan behind and Abbi, firmly clutching Joe's hand, in the rear.

"I can't come," Jenna said. "I have to practise."

"You always say that," Abbi complained. "It's not like you really have to practise, the way I have to look after Joe!" She gave Joe's hand an angry tug.

"Let go of me!" he protested.

"Oh, no! I'm not letting you out of my clutches until we're safe at home," Abbi cried.

"You guys don't understand," Jenna frowned. "I have to practise every day or I'll stiffen up…"

"Hey, what happened to your dance workshop?" Dan said suddenly. "I thought you and Matt were supposed to be with the famous Jared Wesker."

They all stopped and stared at Matt and Jenna.

"We were," Jenna shrugged. "It didn't work out." She could tell Matt was listening, ahead of her. The tops of his ears were pink.

"What happened?" Lauren turned to ask.

"It just wasn't…what we thought it was…" Jenna ended lamely. She could see Matt's shoulders relax. He was glad she wasn't talking about the way he had run out of the workshop. I won't tell, Jenna thought. It will just be between us.

☆CHAPTER NINE☆

Real Money!

Jenna's mother greeted her at the door of their house. Her black eyes were sparkling and her whole face was alive with pleasure. "I've just had the most amazing phone call–" she began.

"I know, Mum. It was someone from the Lara Lake Modelling Agency, right?"

"You don't sound very excited for a girl that's just been offered a four figure contract," Mrs James said.

"Four figures?" Jenna collapsed on the hall stairs.

"Isn't it exciting," her mother smiled. "They want you to come for photographs and a try-out next week."

"But I'm rehearsing every day for the New York dance competition..." Jenna said, "for a scholarship."

"I know," her mother waved her hand. "Let's not talk about it now. You look like you've been working too hard. You look tired. Go and rest, now. Joyce and I are cooking something special."

"I'm not tired," Jenna thumped up the stairs. She hated it when her mother acted as if too much dancing would wear her out, or something. And now she would start pressuring her about this modelling business. She knew that look on her mum's face only too well!

☆

"Why wouldn't you jump at a chance to be a model?" Joyce shook her head at dinner. "For once you wouldn't have to worry all the time about your height. They want you to be tall. The taller the better!"

"I know," Jenna mumbled. She pushed her beans around on her plate, not eating.

"And there's real money in modelling," Joyce went on, "not like dance. I read that dancers are paid worse than street sweepers."

"I just can't believe you think I should be a model," Jenna flashed. "You're always saying dance is just showing off. What do you think modelling is?"

"Well, at least they pay you well for it!" Joyce snorted. "You wouldn't have to work for scholarships if you had modelling fees."

"I don't think you should make a decision until you've had a chance to think about it," Jenna's mum told her. "And whatever Joyce and I might think – it's still your decision."

But her mother still had that hopeful look, Jenna thought, as she went upstairs after dinner. Money was tight in their household. The roof needed fixing, her mum needed a new car, and they hadn't been back to Grenada to see her grandparents for years. Her mum hadn't said all those things, but she didn't have to. It was in her eyes.

Jenna flopped on her bed. Her whole life felt like it was falling apart. She and Matt didn't even have a dance for the competition yet, and even if they did, they couldn't dance together. The chances of winning that scholarship were zero!

There was a gentle knock on her door.

"Yes?" Jenna called.

Her mother poked her head in the door. "Can I come in?"

"Sure." Jenna sat up, hugging her pillow.

"I'm sorry if we got carried away," Jenna's mother sighed. "I'm just so proud of you. You've grown into a beautiful young woman – so beautiful that sometimes I hardly recognize my little girl."

"But…" Jenna began.

"I know you've grown so fast that you hardly know yourself, and that makes you self-conscious," Jenna's mum went on. "That's why it's nice when other people pick you out in a crowd and say, 'Look at that girl!' Your father would be so proud."

Jenna gulped. Her mum almost never talked about her dad. Jenna wished she would, but her mum always got emotional when she mentioned him. Like now. The tears were shining in her mother's eyes.

Jenna took her hand. "The thing is, Mum, I don't just want to be looked at." She took a deep breath; "I want to dance. I want to make people feel that special feeling when I'm dancing, as if they're flying…"

Her mother nodded. "I know. I just worry…"

"What do you worry about?" Jenna felt irritated again. It was so hard to talk to Mum!

"That you'll work, and work, and…" her mother fumbled for words.

"And never be a great dancer? That's what you mean, isn't it?"

"No, I don't mean that. You'll do whatever you set out to do, I'm sure," her mum sighed. "Even as a two-year-old you ran everywhere on your toes. I could never keep up. It's just that I'd like you to keep your options open."

Jenna hugged her back. She knew her mum was trying to understand, but she didn't really. Jenna didn't want options. She was totally dedicated to dancing.

Right now, she really needed to get out of this house. She reached for her jacket and ran out of the room.

"Can I go over to Lauren's?" she called to her mother. "I'll be home before eight."

Her mother hurried out into the hall. "I'm sure you want to talk to your friends about this big decision," she smiled. "Go ahead."

☆CHAPTER TEN☆

Telling Lies

Lauren lived in a big house on a quiet, tree-lined street. Imagine having this much space! Jenna stretched out both her long slender arms in the front hall as she waited for Lauren. At home she could touch both walls if she reached out like this.

Lauren came down the carpeted stairway.

"Hi, Jenna," she said shyly. "Come on up to my room."

There was another large hall at the top of the stairs, with doors on both sides. Lauren's room was enormous, with a high ceiling and a big bed in the middle. There was a seat under the window, and a comfortable chair.

Jenna stood still for a moment, taking in all this luxury. Deep carpets, a matching bedspread, curtains with pink roses, and a bookshelf crammed with books.

"I love your room," she said sincerely. For some reason, she thought about the modelling contract. It would buy all this!

"It's the only place they leave me alone," Lauren said. "If I go downstairs, my mother or father or brother are always bugging me about practising the piano or my singing, about why I'm wasting my talent…" her voice trailed off. "Let's not talk about that."

"No," Jenna agreed. "I came to talk about Matt."

This time the flush on Lauren's cheeks was instant and painful. She collapsed on the window seat and stared out of the window.

"The other day…" Jenna stumbled on, "I think you thought I was trying to…that maybe I liked Matt. But I was just trying to convince him to go to the dance workshop."

Lauren was still looking out of the window. This wasn't going well.

"I don't like him…" Jenna fumbled for the right words. "It's not my fault that Miss Adaman made us partners."

"I know," Lauren whispered.

"We don't get along," said Jenna. "We fight all the time. He drives me crazy!"

"It's OK." Lauren looked up.

"Really?" Jenna sat in the armchair and looked hard at her friend's face.

"Yes, really. He told me about the dance workshop. I said he should go," Lauren sighed. "It's hopeless, anyway. He just thinks of me as sweet little Lauren."

Jenna shook her head. "He talks about you all the time. Lauren this…Lauren that. He loves the way you sing."

Lauren's face flushed. "How is your dance for the competition coming along?" she asked, changing the subject away from her.

"Terrible," Jenna admitted. "I wish I could just get Matt to work a little bit. He could be so good, if he tried."

"Winning the scholarship means a lot to you, doesn't it?" said Lauren.

"It would mean everything," Jenna said eagerly. "It would mean I might really have a career in dance. Otherwise..." she broke off.

"What?" Lauren looked anxiously into her face.

"Otherwise I might as well just give up and be a model, or something," Jenna said.

"A model?" Lauren looked startled. "What gave you that idea?"

Jenna found herself telling Lauren about being 'discovered' and the contract. "My mum really wants me to go along for the photo shoot, I can tell," she said.

"Oh, you can't!" Lauren breathed. "You've worked so hard. You're a dancer, Jenna. You've got to dance! Listen, I'll help, I promise. I'll bug Matt until he promises to work."

Jenna grinned gratefully at her friend. "Thanks," she said. "Even if it doesn't work, thanks for believing in me."

She looked round the large room, now wrapped in shadows. "I wish I had a room like this," she said. "I could really practise in here."

"It's sort of lonely sometimes," Lauren told her. "I wish you lived closer. You could come here and rehearse. I've got some neat books about dancers – would you like to see them?"

☆**55**☆

Half an hour later, Jenna ran down the stairs to Lauren's front door with an armload of books. There were biographies of Danilova and Pavlova, two great Russian ballerinas. There was a photo book of Nureyev, and another of American ballerinas.

"Bring them back whenever you want," Lauren called. "I don't need them."

Jenna clutched her armful of treasures. "Thanks, Lauren!" The twisted feeling inside was gone. So she had told a lie about not liking Matt. Lauren meant more to her than Matt and all his charm and good looks. She could never hurt her friend.

So, forget him! she told herself firmly, for the tenth time that day.

☆

After dinner, Matt strolled out to the garden behind his tall narrow townhouse. It was just a small square of black earth now, but next spring the place would be a riot of tomato plants, climbing beans and grape vines on an arbour. Every centimetre of space would grow vegetables.

Matt sat on the porch rail and swung his feet. The house had been this way since his grandfather had come from Italy and started Caruso Brothers. His father had been a little boy, when they arrived, and he had grown up to take over the store.

Soon it will be my turn, Matt thought, unless I become a famous dancer in the meantime. He smiled to himself. That would never happen! His parents didn't mind him dancing, as long as he knew that someday he'd be the third Caruso to be in the fruit and vegetable business.

If they thought he was serious about a career as a dancer…

Matt hopped down off the rail into the soft dirt. He paced out the yard, placing one foot carefully in front of the other, balancing with his arms out. The yard was just under ten metres long, and six wide.

His whole world. Suddenly, Matt felt restless. Such a little world. He ran back up the porch steps, and shook the mud off his shoes.

"What are you doing?" his mother called from the open kitchen window. "Take off those shoes before you track dirt on my clean floor!"

"Sure, Ma!" Matt shouted back. He took off his shoes and started down the stairs to his own private room in the basement.

"Matt, can you come and play with us?" His little sister had heard him come in.

"Later!" Matt bellowed. "I have to rehearse!" He put a dance tape in the portable CD player and practised a few warm-up exercises. All at once, he felt a mad urge to leap and turn and soar. He jumped – crashing his head against a ceiling pipe. Luckily, it was loose, and shifted when he struck it, but the blow still brought tears to his eyes.

Matt collapsed on the floor. Too small, too low, too crowded. If he went upstairs his younger sister and brother would want him to play. Or Dad would have a job for him.

Dad always had a job. Work was all he knew. Even when he wasn't working in the store, he was always working in the garden or fixing the house. Which was why Matt was sure he wanted a life where there was room for other things.

In his mind he began to work out a dance routine. A dance about being trapped in a small world, and reaching out for a bigger one. Jenna could be in it too – they could use their height – as if suddenly everything was too small for them.

Matt began to dance in the small basement space. Everywhere they moved they'd meet walls, and a low ceiling...he'd try to lift her, but there would be no room above them...

He thought about Jenna and the man from the modelling agency. Matt imagined how the man in black would appear in the dance – offering Jenna a way out, opening a door for her.

Suddenly Matt had a creepy feeling. The man in black had an evil grin. He was too smooth, too confident. He was leading Jenna into danger.

Matt shook himself, and switched off the music. He was letting his imagination run away with him. Jenna probably wouldn't like his ideas anyway. She never did!

☆CHAPTER ELEVEN☆

I Have to be Perfect!

Jenna woke up the next morning determined to put Matt and modelling out of her mind and work even harder at her dancing. Before breakfast she practised for an hour in her room. At school, she was in the studio an hour before class, drilling the basic steps, over and over again.

Miss Adaman came over to her at the barre. "That's enough, Jenna," she ordered. "You will hurt yourself." She looked closely at Jenna's face. "You look pale. Are you eating enough?"

"Of course!" Jenna panted. "And I can't stop now. I haven't got this jeté right, yet. It's not quite perfect. It has to be perfect."

"You must take time to look after yourself, I know how you're feeling–" Miss Adaman began.

"No, you don't!" Jenna flared, then caught herself. "I'm sorry Miss Adaman. I know you're a dancer, too." Jenna knew her teacher had torn her knee ligament and had surgery. "But things are so complicated."

"And dance is so simple..." Miss Adaman sighed. "When it's perfect you feel like you can control the universe. But you can't force it, Jenna. Part of becoming a dancer is allowing your body to grow."

"I have grown enough," Jenna laughed bitterly. "If I get any taller I can't be a ballerina." She looked down at her long slim legs. "I've got to win this scholarship, Miss Adaman."

At that moment, Matt breezed in, whistling cheerfully. "Hi," he grinned at Jenna. "Ready to work?"

Jenna felt the familiar mix of anger and laughter that Matt always made her feel. She put her hands on her hips. "The question is...are you?"

There was a serious glint behind the laughter in Matt's eyes as they warmed up together. "Did the modelling agency call your mother?" he asked as they bent and stretched side by side to the music.

Jenna nodded.

"And?" Matt asked.

"My mum and sister already have me walking down the catwalks in Paris and Milan," Jenna said.

"And you still don't want to try for it?" Matt asked.

"This is what I want to do." Jenna stretched with one leg over her head.

"Then let's dance. I have some ideas for the competition piece. See if you like them."

Matt sketched his ideas by dancing them.

How did he understand her so perfectly? Jenna wondered. That was exactly how life felt to her right now, as though she were in a cage, a space that didn't fit.

She added her own ideas. "We can dance the roles that people try to force us to into," she said. "I'll dance being a model, looking in a mirror, tied up in tight clothes, posing for those fake fashion photographs." She struck a pose.

"And I'll throw footballs, and lug you around like a crate of lettuce," Matt laughed. "Just like Wesker said I did."

"He didn't understand you," the words were out of Jenna's mouth before she could stop them. Matt stared at her.

"But Lauren understands you," Jenna said quickly, glancing away. "She thinks you're marvellous."

They had stopped dancing and were standing, centimetres away from each other.

"She'd really like it if you went to the Celtic concert on Sunday," Jenna went on.

"I think we should all go," Matt said. "Lauren's one of the gang."

Jenna breathed a sigh of relief. The tense moment was over and things were back to normal. They were all just part of the gang.

☆

The noise in the canteen was deafening. Jenna and Matt joined the others at their usual table with trays of food and cans of cold drink. Dan, as usual, had his brown paper bag and two cheese sandwiches.

"Don't you ever eat anything else?" Matt asked him.

"Why should I?" Dan grinned. "There's nothing better than bread and cheese. You guys gum up your insides with all that guck..." he motioned to the chips and fried food. "I'll stick to my sandwiches. What's new?" Dan asked, to change the subject.

"Joe's driving me bananas," Abbi said. "He knows I can't tell Mum about him, because I never told her we were going to the fair. I don't know what to do with him."

"Bring him to Lauren's concert on Sunday," Matt said. "We'll all help you keep an eye on him."

"I'd have to get a leash for the little monster," Abbi groaned, her head in her hands.

"Hey, Jenna, aren't you going to tell them your news?" Matt teased.

"What?" Abbi sat straight up. "What happened, Jen?"

"It's nothing," Jenna shrugged.

"She was discovered, right on Main Street. Picked out of the crowd by a roving talent scout," Matt laughed. "And she says it's nothing."

"Tell us," Dan said. "You have to, now that Matt's opened his big mouth."

Jenna told them about the man from Lara Lake and the photo shoot. She didn't mention the possible money, but she didn't have to.

"Wow!" Abbi's eyes were glowing. "Do you realize what this means? Money, buckets of money. Your picture on the cover of hundreds of magazines. Travel, jets to here, jets to there. Beaches...cosmetic contracts...clothes...oh, Jenna!" Abbi longed to be famous.

"But Jenna doesn't want all that," Lauren said.

"She's crazy," Matt put his arm around Lauren's shoulder. "She thinks it will interfere with dancing—"

"But Jenna!" Abbi cried.

"You could still dance…" Dan added.

Jenna was having trouble hearing them. Her attention was totally focused on Matt's arm, draped on Lauren's shoulder. The ache inside was back, worse than before. "I just don't want to be a model," she said. "It might mean I would have to leave the school."

The others were quiet for a moment.

"But how can you say no?" Abbi burst out. "Couldn't you just try it and see what happened? You have to start young if you want to be a top model…"

"Or a dancer." Jenna shook her head.

"Poor Jenna," Lauren said. "It must be so hard to decide."

"At least with acting, you can wait till your twenties or thirties to start," Dan agreed.

"The same with singing," Lauren nodded.

"So, speaking of singing, we're all coming to the Celtic concert, right?" Matt looked around at the others. He smiled into Lauren's wide grey eyes. "I want to hear you sing some more."

Jenna stood up suddenly. "I have to go," she said. "See you later." Matt still had his arm around Lauren. She couldn't look at them.

The others watched her walk away through the crowded canteen.

"Wow!" Abbi said. "I wish someone would offer me the chance to model. Then I could hire a babysitter for Joe."

"What about Lauren's concert?" Dan asked hopefully. "Can you come on Sunday?"

Abbi nodded. "I'm going to ask Mum to find someone else to look after Joe," she said.

"I'm sure Jenna will come, too." Matt looked after Jenna. He wished he knew why she had got so prickly all of a sudden. Maybe he shouldn't have blabbed about the modelling contract.

Lauren felt happiness fizzing up inside her. She could have sat forever at the canteen table, beside Matt, with his arm around her shoulders.

☆CHAPTER TWELVE☆

Celtic Concert

The phone rang while Jenna was on her way upstairs after school. She hurried back down and picked up the receiver.

"May I speak to Jenna James, please?" She recognized the rough, gravelly voice immediately. It was Norman Mars, from the modelling agency.

"Have you decided whether you're interested? I have a slot next week when I could fit you in for a photo shoot."

Jenna wanted to say, "No, I'm not interested," and hang up. Her tight, perfectly controlled world of dance seemed to be falling apart. First, Matt, and now Norman Mars were trying to break it down. But she could see the faces of her friends – the mixture of admiration and excitement when they heard the news about the modelling contract.

"I uh...don't know," she mumbled.

"Well, we could do it Wednesday at seven thirty, if you're free?" Norman said.

"Seven thirty in the morning?" Jenna asked.

"Great heavens, girl, no!" There was a laugh on the other end of the phone. "Seven thirty in the evening. I'm never up before eleven. Call me back if that suits you…Check it out with your mother."

He knows my mother approves, Jenna thought as she hung up the phone. He's talking like I've decided to come already.

She went up the stairs more slowly, thinking hard. Nine girls out of ten her age would be dazed with delight to have such a chance at fame and fortune. Jenna had seen their pictures in magazines – Five Hot New Faces. It was supposed to be every girl's dream. But I already have a dream, Jenna thought. What am I going to do?

When the phone rang again, Jenna raced down the stairs, ready to tell Norman Mars to stop pestering her.

But it was not the talent scout. It was Matt.

"Hey, Jenna," his voice was warm and friendly. "So, are you coming on Sunday night?"

"I…don't know," Jenna stammered.

"I called to talk you into it," Matt said. "You need some fun in your drab life, some time with your friends."

"But I–"

"No 'buts'. I've been trying to work at my dancing."

"I know. I'm glad."

"So…" Matt went on, "…so you have to work at having a life. Lauren will be disappointed if we're not all there."

"All right!" Jenna heard herself laugh. "I'll be there."

☆

The Roxy Theatre where the Lilith Singers were going to perform was an old movie theatre converted to a concert hall. The stage was small, the seats ancient but comfortable.

By the time Matt, Jenna, Dan and Abbi arrived, the seats on the main floor were mostly filled.

"Good crowd!" Dan whistled.

"Let's go up to the balcony." Abbi raced towards the stairs. "We can sit together and still get a good view."

They trooped up the stairs to the old theatre balcony and found seats in the first row.

"Will Lauren be able to see us up here?" Matt wondered.

"I don't think so. The lights will be in her eyes." Dan craned his neck to look at the bank of lights behind them.

All at once the lights went out, and the soft sounds of a harp and a hammered dulcimer could be heard from backstage. The lights went up, and the Lilith Singers walked on stage in single file, dressed as though they were on a pilgrimage, with William the piper leading the procession.

At the end of the line came a slender figure dressed in a simple white dress that fell like a column from her neck to her feet. It was tied around her waist with a green cord.

"Look at Lauren!" Matt breathed.

She was small and incredibly remote-looking in her white gown, like a person from another world.

"Wow, I've never seen her like that," Matt whispered. "She's beautiful!"

The line of performers began to sing a round, with one part beginning the song, then another section joining in, and finally a third. As the song ended, Lauren's section was the last to be heard.

"Listen!" Matt said. "You can hear Lauren's voice above the others."

Abbi dug him in the ribs with her elbow. "Be quiet, Matt!" she hissed. "We can all hear. We'd like to listen to the music!"

But Matt was too excited to sit still. He leaned on the balcony rail, straining forward to hear every note, then flung himself back into his seat when the song ended. "Man," he said. "I wish they'd let Lauren sing by herself."

Jenna felt paralysed. On one hand, she was thrilled to see and hear Lauren perform, on the other she was burning with that old twisting pain, every time Matt said something else about how beautiful Lauren was, or how well she sang.

I'm jealous! she thought with astonishment. I'm jealous of Lauren, because Matt likes her. What kind of a friend am I? If she could have run away, she would have, but she felt frozen to her seat.

When it was finally over, they clapped and whistled and hooted from the balcony, then all trooped backstage to congratulate Lauren.

"Hi!" William greeted them, his long face breaking into a big grin. "Where's your little brother today?" he asked Abbi.

"I left him at home," Abbi said. "Good thing, too. He'd get into trouble here, for sure. Look at it – this is a real theatre!"

She was gazing around the busy backstage area, with its ropes and flats and dusty props. The others recognized the look on her face. Abbi was completely stage-struck.

"That was a brilliant performance!" Matt was shaking Lauren's hand. "Could you hear us cheering our heads off?"

"My palms are still red from clapping!" Dan showed her.

Lauren laughed. "You might have overdone it, but thanks." She bowed in her long dress.

"We've been trying to persuade Lauren to tour with us at Christmas," William said. "We do a series of concerts in churches and shopping malls."

Lauren's face was glowing. "Jenna," she whispered as they put on their coats. "Thank you for getting Matt to come."

"Matt called and made me come," Jenna laughed shakily. "He wanted to be here."

"I think he finally noticed me…as a girl," Lauren was bubbling with happiness.

"Well, of course he did. You look stunning," Jenna said. She was trying to sound sincere, but inside her stomach was churning.

"I'll see you tomorrow," Lauren squeezed her arm. "Thank you for being such a good friend."

Jenna didn't feel like a real friend. She was trying to be happy for Lauren. Everything was working out better than she'd ever dreamed. But inside, Jenna felt a storm of unhappiness and guilt. She wanted to leave the theatre and fling herself back into the world of dance, where everything was neat and orderly and she had perfect control!

☆

Jenna ran up the steps and unlocked her front door. Her room, with its homemade ballet barre beckoned. She dumped her dance bag and headed up the stairs.

"Jenna, is that you?" Her mother appeared from the back of the house.

No, it's not Jenna, it's a total stranger bursting into your house. Who do you think it is? Jenna wanted to shout, but she controlled herself with a deep breath. "What?" she said, trying to make it sound polite.

"I checked into that modelling agency, through the library." Her mother had been in the kitchen working at her accounts on the kitchen table. "I decided I'd better find out if they were legitimate."

"And?" Jenna tried again not to sound impatient.

"Well, they seem very legitimate," her mother smiled. "They have branches in several countries, an international reputation, high standards…"

"Thanks, Mum," Jenna said, tight-lipped.

"So, if you wanted to…I mean if you change your mind…"

"Thanks," Jenna said again. "I'd like to go up to my room now, if that's OK." Two seconds more and she was going to explode.

"It's OK," her mother smiled. "I realize it's a lot to take in, at your age – a big decision."

She says that as if she knows I'll make the right decision, Jenna thought, as she finally fled to the safety of her room.

☆CHAPTER THIRTEEN☆

Escape Artist

When Abbi got home from the concert she found the babysitter, Mrs Murgatroyd, sitting in front of the TV, sobbing.

"What's wrong?' Abbi cried.

"It's Lucy." Mrs Murgatroyd wiped her eyes. She's just broken up with Troy…"

"You're watching a soap!" Abbi cried. "Where's Joe?"

Mrs Murgatroyd pointed in the direction of Joe's bedroom. She never moved unless she had to, and she was addicted to television, but she was the only person they could get to look after Joe.

"How long has he been in there?" Abbi asked her.

"Oh, dear, I don't know. There was *General Hospital*, and then *Coronation Street*, and *The Young and the Restless*…I brought the tapes of all my shows."

Abbi went down the hall to Joe's room.

The POW-KAPOW!! of a video game sound-track was loud, even with the door closed. He'd never hear her knock.

Abbi opened the door. The room was dark, except for the flashing, pulsing, coloured light from the screen.

"Joe?" Abbi called.

There was no answer. Abbi looked around. "You little monster – where are you hiding? In the cupboard? Under the bed? Behind the curtains?"

Joe wasn't in any of his usual hiding spots. His room was empty.

Abbi dashed down the hall. He wasn't in the bathroom, or the kitchen. The doors to her room and her mother's were open and a quick search told her that those rooms, too, were empty!

Abbi stood in the hall, her thoughts whirling. "Mrs Murgatroyd!" she bellowed at the babysitter. "Did you see Joe go out?"

"No, dear, he's in his room, playing video games," Mrs Murgatroyd repeated, as if her mind was on endless playback.

It would be easy for Joe to slip out, Abbi thought. Mrs M. wouldn't notice unless someone pulled out the cable for the television set.

Abbi quietly slipped out of the apartment door. She thought she knew where Joe might be. All the way down the stairs she was praying she would find him.

She ran through the big, echoing lobby of the building and out onto the street. At the corner was a small store that had video games in the back.

As Abbi approached she saw three teenage guys, older than herself, leaving the store. One handed the other a small paper packet. Drugs!

Abbi thought, turning her eyes away. The store was a dealers' hang-out!

Abbi burst through the door of the shop. At the back was a crowd of boys, and in the middle of them she saw spikes of red hair.

"What are you doing here?" she shouted at Joe, dragging him by the coat sleeve away from a space aliens video game.

"Hey! Stop! I'm winning – oh, great, I have the best score in Space Tigers I've ever had, and you come along and wreck it."

"Hey, Joe, is that your big sister?" one of the guys laughed.

"Looks like you're in trouble now," another jeered.

"You're supposed to be at home with Mrs M. What are you doing here?' Abbi repeated.

"I got bored!" Joe's blue eyes stared into Abbi's own. "I hate sitting up in the apartment with smelly old Mrs M."

"Wait till Mum hears about this!" Abbi dragged her furious little brother out of the store. Behind him, the guys were laughing.

"You'd better not tell," Joe said, twisting out of her grip, trying to get away. "I've got lots to tell about you."

"Go ahead!" Abbi said furiously. "This is serious, Joe. You shouldn't be hanging around that place."

"Why not, all my friends are there."

They had reached their building. Abbi shoved Joe through the doors. "Those guys are too old for you. They're into drugs and things." Abbi shook her head. "I saw them…"

"Please don't tell Mum!" Now Joe looked scared. "I'll do anything. I promise I won't go back."

Abbi shook her head again. She didn't know what to do. Joe was becoming more and more difficult every day. He didn't listen to Mum, he was in trouble at school. She was the only person he seemed to talk to.

If I tell on him, Abbi thought, he'll have nobody he can trust.

☆CHAPTER FOURTEEN☆

Taking Steps

The dance studio was on the top floor of William S. Holly. As she hurried up the final flight of stairs, Jenna was determined not to let her feelings or thoughts of modelling interfere with her dancing. There was only a week before the competition.

But as soon as she saw Matt, her determination turned to dust. He was warming up at the barre, chattering to the other students at the same time, a better dancer than any of them, and trying half as hard.

"Hi, Jen!" He waved at her in the mirror.

Jenna flopped down on a bench to put on her dance shoes. Her hands were shaking as she did up the laces.

"I'd like to see how your competition dances are coming along." Miss Adaman stood in the centre of the floor. "After warm-ups, get with your partner, and let's run through them."

Jenna found a place at the barre as far from Matt as possible. Dance conversation drifted around her as she went through the familiar warm-up routine.

She was concentrating fiercely when Matt came up and put his hands on her waist and stood behind her. Their two faces were reflected in the mirror, side by side.

"Notice how I was here early?" he grinned at her reflection. "Before you, even!"

Jenna could feel her whole body shaking.

"What's wrong?" Matt said quickly.

"Oh, it's that modelling thing," Jenna said. "I don't know what to do, that's all." She wished he wouldn't stand so close, and smile at her that way.

"So, are you ready to knock Miss Adaman dead with our great routine?" Matt asked.

Jenna nodded, unable to speak.

"Know what I like about our dance?" Matt said. "No lifts. None of this towering hulk helpless female stuff."

Jenna managed a shaky grin. Trust Matt to put a positive spin on the fact that he couldn't lift her very well. Hopefully the dance competition judges would see it that way.

They watched the other pairs of dancers go through their routines. Some were good, others just OK. None of them seemed to have the energy or imagination of theirs.

"Jenna and Matt, are you ready?"

They looked at each other. The music began.

Something was wrong. As soon as she and Matt were face to face, Jenna stumbled awkwardly. She felt paralysed, as though her body was not attached to her head.

"Jenna?" Miss Adaman held up her hand for the

music to stop. "Are you all right?'

Matt's face was full of concern.

"I'm fine," Jenna said fiercely. There was a moment's pause and the music began again.

Once again, Jenna's steps were awkward, out of control. The room felt as if it were spinning.

Miss Adaman stopped the music and hurried over. "Are you ill, dear?" she asked kindly.

"No, I–" Jenna gulped.

"Can we have a minute alone, Matt?" Miss Adaman said, and Matt, his face furrowed into a worried frown, left them.

Miss Adaman looked sternly into Jenna's face. "Is it Matt?"

"No, it's not Matt. I just…can't dance today."

"I think you should consider dropping out of the scholarship competition," Miss Adaman said. "You've been driving yourself too hard, Jenna. This was bound to happen."

Jenna drew in a big breath. "I'm fine," she said, looking Miss Adaman straight in the eye.

But she wasn't fine. Something was happening to her, something terrible. She could not stay focused! She was a mess! The slightest touch of Matt's hand, a glance from his dark eyes, threw her off balance, made her knees turn to jelly. It was as if all the years of practice to be perfect meant nothing! Now she knew why Matt always made her feel so prickly and out of sorts – it was because she really liked him! She couldn't dance because her feelings were getting in the way. I'll never be a great dancer, Jenna thought. I've been fooling myself all this time!

"Take a rest. No more dancing today, and think seriously about the competition." Mary Adaman said, "You have to keep dancing in perspective – it's not your whole life. I want to talk to you more about this, but I have to go on with the class. Come and see me afterwards."

Jenna nodded, but all she really wanted was to get out of the studio. Her safe perfect world of dance was crumbling. She got her bag and slipped out of the studio doors.

Today was the day Norman Mars had said he had time for the photo shoot. There was still time to make an appointment. If she couldn't be a dancer, she could at least be a model, and make her mother happy!

Jenna headed for the pay phone at the end of the hall.

She found the business card in her pack and shakily dialled the number.

"I'd like to speak to Norman, please," she told the female voice that answered the phone.

"Can I say who's calling?"

"It's Jenna…Jennifer James."

"I'll see if Mr Mars is available." Jenna was put on hold. There was jazz in the background.

She looked up and there was Matt, staring at her.

"What are you doing?" he said.

Jenna waved him away.

Norman Mars was on the phone. "Jenna?"

"If there's still an opening tonight, I'd like to

come," Jenna said. "Seven thirty...what's the address?" She held the phone under her chin and wrote on the back of the business card against the wall. "I'll be there."

"That's fantastic," Norman said. "By next week at this time you could be on your way to New York for a shoot!"

"Um...I see. All right, I'll see you tonight."

Jenna hung up.

Matt's brown eyes were full of questions.

"I'm going to try for the modelling thing," Jenna said. Now that she'd made the decision it was easier to breathe. She just had to get away from Matt, from his questioning eyes.

"That's good...I think."

"I have to get my pictures taken tonight. I could start work next week," Jenna went on.

"Next week? That's the dance competition!"

"I'm not dancing so well, and Miss Adaman thinks maybe I should drop out and take a rest," Jenna shrugged. "And you don't really care..."

There was a note of anger in Matt's voice. "I don't care about winning the competition, but I was starting to like our dance. What made you change your mind? Was it my lousy dancing? I have been trying."

Matt's usually teasing eyes were serious.

Jenna looked away. "I know you've been trying. It's me. I'll never be a dancer. I might as well take this chance while I have it."

"What do you mean you'll never be a dancer? You're already a terrific dancer!"

"I'm just not tough enough to take the pressure…" Jenna gulped. This was awful. Why didn't Matt go away?

The bell rang for the end of class. Doors banged open and the hall filled with noisy, running kids.

"I've got to go," Jenna said.

"Me too…" Matt said, his forehead creased with worry. "Look, I'll see you in the canteen, later. I want to talk to you…" As he took off down the hall, weaving and bobbing through the traffic of bodies, Jenna looked after him.

Always before, when she had felt lost and confused, dancing had been her refuge. Now where could she go?

☆CHAPTER FIFTEEN☆

Jenna Caves In

"I've never seen Jenna like that." Matt tossed his equipment bag on a chair and sat down next to Lauren at the canteen table.

"What's wrong?" Lauren asked, feeling the familiar beating of her heart whenever Matt sat close to her.

"Oh, you know. She's usually so strong and sure of herself – the woman warrior. But today she just caved when we had a little trouble with our dance for the competition." Matt shook his head. "She's talking about dropping out of the competition. She's going to try that modelling thing."

Lauren's grey eyes were wide. "Oh, no. She doesn't really want to do that!"

"It's like she's given up." Matt shook his head. "I wish I knew what was wrong."

Lauren's mind was racing. She had caught a glimpse of Matt's real feelings about Jenna. Underneath all the jokes and teasing he liked her a lot!

Lauren gulped. "What are you going to do?"

"I don't know." Matt twisted unhappily in his

chair. "I don't like her going to that photo shoot by herself. There was something kind of creepy about that Mars guy…"

"Jenna can look after herself…" Lauren started to say.

"Oh, I know, she acts cool and tough," Matt stood up. "But she's different today, as if she didn't care what happened!"

Just then, Dan and Abbi came up to the table. Abbi's cloud of hair was pulled back in a tight bun. Dan was looking apologetic.

"Abbi, I'm sorry…" His comic face had a sad clown mouth.

"It's not your fault! Why couldn't I see? Why? Why?"

When Abbi was being dramatic, there was no one more theatrical. She threw herself down on a chair and the air around her pulsed with misery.

Lauren and Matt exchanged glances. Somebody had to say it. "What couldn't you see?" Lauren asked.

"I can't talk about it!" Abbi put her tragic head down on her arms.

"We did a role-playing scene," said Dan with a sigh. "Abbi played her brother Joe. I was their mother. It got pretty wild."

"I was Joe, having this fight with Mum," Abbi pulled the clip off her hair, and her gold-blonde curls cascaded around her face. "Suddenly, I was saying all this stuff about how I needed my father, I needed him to love me, I needed to be with him…and I was crying…"

"I was Abbi's mum, promising to try to find the money to send Joe with Abbi to Australia this summer," Dan explained.

"Sometimes you can discover the truth through acting," Abbi said. "I'll write to my dad and somehow make him see that Joe needs to come to Australia as badly as I do. We have to find the money."

"Money," Dan sighed with a sorrowful shrug. "It always comes back to that!"

Matt was looking thoughtful. "Maybe that's Jenna's problem," he said hurriedly. "Maybe her family is broke, and she's going to try modelling for the money!"

☆

"I won't tell Mum and Joyce I'm going to the photo shoot," Jenna said to herself. "They'll just get their hopes up."

Secretly, Jenna didn't want to explain her sudden change of heart. It would be easy to get out tonight, get to the photo shoot and be home before they missed her. Mum worked late at the library, and Joyce had night classes on Monday nights. Neither of them would be home until eleven.

Jenna was too nervous to eat. What should I wear? she wondered. Models always wore extreme clothes – high heels and lots of make up. She pored over the clothes in her cupboard, then Joyce's.

Joyce had black boots with heels – they might be good. Jenna found some black opaque tights and a short skirt and tried them on with the boots.

She looked at herself in the mirror.

Her baggy old tunics and sweat shirts weren't going to match that! She borrowed one of her mother's neat white shirts. There! When she checked her image again she looked older, and more sophisticated.

She stuffed a few more of her sister's tops into her dance bag and a silky purple dress that Joyce had once worn to a wedding.

Jenna glanced at the clock in the hall as she ran downstairs. Almost seven. She should make it to Norman Mars' studio just in time. Being on time was important!

☆CHAPTER SIXTEEN☆

Sudden Discoveries

By the time the bus dropped her off on the corner of Duncan Avenue, Jenna was almost late. It had taken longer than she thought to get here. The building was a converted furniture factory with high, brick, ivy-covered walls.

Jenna walked down the darkening street from the bus stop and paused in front of the building. The entrance seemed to be down a long passageway under an arched gate.

There were heaps of rubbish on both sides of the passage – ruined mattresses, empty paint cans, plastic and wood rubble.

When she got to the door and read the names on the bent and broken mailboxes, she wondered if she was in the right building. There was a men's gym, a giftware company, and some artists' studios. This couldn't be where the Lara Lake Modelling Agency had their offices, Jenna thought. There must be some mistake!

She read the address on the back of the business card again, by the dim light over the door. It was the right address. Maybe part of the building had been renovated. Maybe there was another entrance.

Jenna glanced anxiously at her watch. Almost seven thirty. She retraced her steps down the rubble-strewn passageway and back to the street. The building was immense. It must cover almost the entire city block.

Jenna began to run down the street at the side of the building, looking for a front entrance.

☆

Matt paced his basement retreat. He couldn't shake off the feeling that something was wrong. Finally, he got up his nerve to phone Jenna's house.

There was no answer.

Matt put down the phone and started pacing again.

Ten minutes later he called the operator and asked for the Lara Lake Modelling Agency number.

"I'd like to speak to Norman Mars," he told the human being he finally reached after listening to two minutes of voice mail messages.

"Mr Mars doesn't work here," came back the breathless voice. "And the offices are closed. I'm teaching a night class – you caught me on my break."

Matt felt a prickle down his spine.

"You don't know a Norman Mars?" He could hear his voice crack.

"Oh, yes, we know him. He's a photographer that does some freelance work for us."

"A friend of mine has a photo shoot with him tonight. That isn't for Lara Lake?"

"It might be," the voice said doubtfully. "He brings in portfolios of prospects sometimes...you know, pictures of girls."

"But he couldn't offer a girl, say, a contract with the agency?" Matt wanted to be perfectly clear.

"Oh, no. He just brings in portfolios, and sometimes he uses our models for assignments."

"Do you know where his studio is?" Matt asked.

"No, I'm afraid I don't. Sorry...Got to go." The line went dead.

Matt stood there with the phone in his hand. Norman Mars had spun a whole fantasy on a thin thread. If Lara Lake liked Jenna's pictures she might take her on. Might. It wasn't a sure thing at all.

"I have to reach Jenna," Matt thought desperately. He called her home again, but the phone rang with the hollow sound of a phone in an empty house.

Matt realized he didn't know where Jenna's mother or sister worked, or how to reach them.

He dived for the phone book, flipping through till he came to the M section. Mars, Mars, Mars...there he was!

Matt picked up the phone to call and then realized — what would he say? I'm on to you, mister? You lied to my friend? It would sound so stupid, and what good would it do?

Matt checked the address in the phone book. 18 Duncan Avenue. It wasn't too far.

His parents were both still working in the store on the corner. Caruso Brothers had a bright green, red and white awning, a cheerful window display of flowers and fresh fruit.

"I finished my homework," Matt said. "I have to go over to Jenna's. We're working on something for school."

"Working?" his father winked. "Working with girls. That's quite a school you're going to."

"I'll be back in an hour." Matt ignored his father's wink. He had very old-fashioned ideas about school and girls.

☆CHAPTER SEVENTEEN☆

'Kodak Moment'

By the time Jenna had run round the entire building, she was sure there were no other entrances. She was breathless and sweaty. And late. Oh, this is great, she told herself. He'll take one look at me and tear up that contract!

Panting, Jenna hurried down the passageway, through a set of dirty glass doors and up a wide wooden stairway. She would find someone in this building who knew where Norman Mars' studio was!

The stairs were creaky and her footsteps echoed up and down the dusty stairwell. On the second floor there was a crude sign, scrawled in red paint on the wall – COLES GYM.

Jenna ran down the hall. It, too, echoed back her footsteps. These ridiculous high-heeled boots, Jenna thought. I sound like a horse.

The gym looked closed for the night, but Jenna could see a light inside. She pounded on the door.

A wide man in a T-shirt and shorts came to the door. "Hey, sister," he said, looking her up and down. "What can I do for you?"

"I'm looking for Norman Mars," Jenna panted. She tried to sound older than thirteen.

"Norman?" the man smiled. "He's on the fifth floor – it's a red door. Can I do anything else for you?"

"No. Thanks," said Jenna.

She ran back along the hall and pounded up three more flights of stairs, pausing to catch her breath in front of the red metal door.

Everything about this place was weird. But she had come this far. She couldn't give up now.

☆

The bus was maddeningly slow. When it got stuck in traffic six blocks from Duncan Avenue, Matt hopped off. He could get there faster on foot.

It was already dark on the cold October night. The streetlights shone on wet concrete as Matt raced down the street, watching the numbers on the buildings. This was a strange part of the city to him.

What must Jenna have thought, he wondered, as he skidded to a stop in front of 18 Duncan Avenue. Surely she wouldn't go in there! The place was a dump.

☆

Jenna pounded on the red door again. This time it was flung open almost immediately. Norman Mars stood there with a camera in his hand. "Hi," he said briefly. "Glad you made it."

"Sorry I'm late," Jenna panted. "I had a little trouble finding your, your…" she peered past the door. A cavernous dark space stretched beyond.

"My loft," Norman finished for her. "Yes, I know, vandals are always coming by and taking the names off the mailboxes. Didn't you see the planet Mars painted on the wall?"

Jenna shook her head.

"Well, never mind, come in. The hair and make-up people aren't here yet, so we have some time to get acquainted. You look like you've been running."

"I know," Jenna smoothed back her hair.

"Never mind, you look fine. Great look! Come in," Norman said again.

Once inside, Jenna could see that the loft was a studio, office and living space rolled into one. Portraits of models hung everywhere.

"What do you think?" Norman asked.

"It's...interesting," Jenna said. She felt like she was in another world. The ceiling was high, a maze of pipes and ducts. Huge windows covered one whole wall of the loft.

"Sit down," Norman said. "Make yourself comfortable. "

Jenna sat on the edge of a leather couch. Norman Mars flipped through a stack of pictures.

"It's hot in the summer, and freezing in the winter," Norman said. "I had a girl in here doing a lingerie shoot in January – she nearly froze to death!"

He pulled out a photograph of a girl in scanty underwear, to show Jenna.

"We were all wearing coats," Norman smiled. "The hair and make-up girls had gloves on, but

Karen was dressed like this! We had to keep stopping to thaw her out. The session took hours!"

Looking at the photo, Jenna suddenly had a strong feeling she shouldn't be here. She was out of her depth. Norman was talking to her and treating her as if she was eighteen or nineteen years old. But he knew she wasn't.

"How long…will this session take?" she asked, trying to keep her voice steady. "I promised my mother I'd be home by nine thirty."

"Oh dear!" Norman looked at his watch. "It's almost eight, already. And it will take nearly an hour to do your hair and make-up…can you call her and see if you can stay longer?"

She couldn't, but Jenna didn't want to admit her mother wasn't home. "I guess it will be all right," she stammered.

"Good," Norman smiled. "You know, usually girls come with their parents. It's nice to see a young woman who is mature enough to handle things on her own. I do find that Mummy sometimes gets in the way."

I've made a stupid mistake, Jenna thought. I've got to get out of here. The realization was like a bucket of water thrown in her face. The girls in the portraits looked at her with blank, grown-up eyes.

Jenna took a deep breath. Somehow, she had to find a way to leave.

"Well," Norman was smiling at her again. "I can't wait to get you in front of the camera. Why don't I shoot a few polaroids, just to get started. Wait here, and I'll just get my things set up."

He disappeared around a partition and Jenna could hear lights being dragged around.

She stood up. It was now or never. "Mr Mars?" Jenna called. "I have to leave now. I forgot something important."

She gave a flying leap for the door, praying it would not be locked. She wrenched it open with a strong tug and fled down the echoing, dusty steps three at a time. As she turned the corner of the first landing, she could hear Norman Mars' door bang and his confused shout: "JENNA, WHERE ARE YOU GOING?"

Then footsteps, pounding down the stairs after her. Jenna was glad she had balance, speed and long legs. If he caught up with her…if she had to explain, she'd die of embarrassment.

She rounded the corner of the main floor and dashed for the doors. OH, NO! Someone was coming in. She could see a shadowy figure through the frosted glass.

Norman Mars was right behind her. She stood, frozen, as someone pulled open the door in front of her.

It was Matt!

"Run!" Jenna gasped, pushing him backwards. Matt grabbed her hand and the two of them streaked through the dark passageway.

"JENNA!" They could hear Norman Mars calling.

"Don't answer," Jenna panted. "Just run!"

☆CHAPTER EIGHTEEN☆

Let's Dance!

"I am so glad to see you!" Jenna panted, as they finally slowed down under a streetlight and she could look at Matt. She started to laugh, shout and snort at the same time. "I guess that was the shortest modelling career in the history of the world!"

"What happened?" Matt was frowning. "He didn't try anything, did he?"

"Oh, no!" Jenna cried. "It was…it was just the whole thing. I suddenly wanted out of there, and I couldn't explain…oh, Matt it was so weird." She was still laughing with relief. The autumn night seemed fresh and alive, and she and Matt were swinging down the street hand in hand.

"What time do you have to get home?" she asked him.

"In an hour or so," Matt said.

"Let's walk," Jenna suggested. "That old bus is so slow and smelly."

"Great," Matt said. It felt natural just walking and holding Jenna's hand. The lights of the tall downtown buildings twinkled above the trees.

"The city is beautiful at night," Jenna said.

"Look, parking meters!"

Matt let go of her hand, ran a few springing steps and hopped over the first meter. In the pool of streetlight he looked like he had wings on his heels.

"Want me to show you how?" he ran back to her.

"Sure," Jenna laughed breathlessly. She realized she wasn't afraid of twisting an ankle, or pulling a ligament. She wanted to fly, like Matt.

"OK, you have to get the timing right. Step, step, step, hands on top of the meter, LIFT!" He showed her. "The important thing is, don't worry, just loosen up and picture yourself zooming over the top."

Jenna took a deep breath. Step, step, step – LIFT! she sang as she flung her body into the air like a gymnast vaulting over a horse. "I did it!" she laughed. "I did it!"

All the way back to Jenna's they flew over fence posts and walked along the tops of narrow benches and did running jumps over grates. They played follow-the-leader, daring each other to mimic one crazy move after another.

At Jenna's, Matt took her hand once more. "Now that," he said, "was dancing!"

"It was…great," Jenna said. "Thanks for coming to the rescue, Matt."

"You didn't need rescuing," Matt laughed. "You were way ahead of old Norman Mars. But if you had, I would have punched him in the nose."

"Thanks," Jenna said. "How did you know where I'd be?"

"I called the agency," Matt explained. "Did you know that slimeball doesn't even work for them? He just takes girls' pictures and then tries to flog them to Lara Lake."

"Oh!" Jenna stared at him, then shook her head. "It figures. Once I was up in his loft, I knew something wasn't right. I should have figured it out as soon as I saw the building, but I was so worried about being on time." She gave Matt a quick hug. "Anyway, it's over. I'm glad I didn't tell my mum...and please don't tell the others at school."

Matt looked embarrassed. "I already told them you were going to the photo shoot. Me and my big mouth."

"Don't worry," Jenna said. "We'll just tell them it turned out to be a scam. Which it was."

"And we're still going to dance for the competition, aren't we?" Matt asked.

"Do you really care?" Jenna asked. She couldn't see Matt's face clearly in the porch light. She felt his hand tighten on hers.

"Yeah, I do. If we have time to practise, I'd like to add some of that follow-the-leader stuff we were just doing."

Jenna grinned in the darkness. She felt good all over – in her body, her mind and her heart. She wanted to be this age and feel this way forever, standing here, holding Matt's hand on an October night, with the smell of fallen leaves all around.

"We'll work it in," she finally said. "See you tomorrow."

☆

Matt went singing into Caruso's Fruit and Vegetables just as his dad was rolling up the awning for the night.

"Well, how did your work go?" his dad asked.

"It was great," Matt said. "Jenna and I might win a scholarship to a dance class in New York this spring."

His father stopped cranking the awning handle. "New York city?" he said. "So you'd be away for a while."

"Just a couple of weeks." Matt took the handle out of his dad's hands to finish cranking up the awning. "If we win…"

☆

The phone was ringing frantically as Jenna walked into the front hall.

"Hello?" she grabbed for it before the person on the other end hung up. It might be her mother.

"Jenna?" It was Lauren. "You sound like you've been running."

Jenna's heart, which had been singing, dropped to the bottom of her sister's high-heeled boots. Lauren!

What about Lauren and Matt?

Which one of them did Matt really like? It was nice of him to rescue me, Jenna thought, but he'd do that for any friend. Underneath all the fooling around, that was the thoughtful, caring kind of person Matt was. She had been so wrong about him!

☆ CHAPTER NINETEEN ☆

Changing Dreams

Three days later, the dance competition was held in William S. Holly's main auditorium.

Lauren slipped into a front seat beside Dan and Abbi. Two circles of colour burned in her cheeks. She hadn't had a chance to talk to Matt since the concert at the Roxy – he had been too busy rehearsing with Jenna. Today, after their dance, she was determined to speak to him privately.

"This is just like when we auditioned..." Abbi whispered in a voice loud enough to be heard two rows back. "Remember how scared we were?"

"I always get nervous when people in our group are performing," Dan added. "It's as if it's me up there instead of Jenna and Matt."

"Oh, I hope they win." Abbi squirmed in her seat. "Jenna's been so worried about Matt not working hard enough for this – but lately he seems to really care, don't you think?"

Lauren could only nod. She didn't trust herself to speak.

And it didn't matter if she said nothing. The others were used to her being silent. Quiet little

Lauren. Mousy little Lauren. Lauren who never got what she wanted because she never asked for what she wanted. But this time, she would let Matt know how she felt, and find out, once and for all, if he felt the same way!

Two minutes later, the dance competition began. They sat through pair after pair, and each one seemed better than the one before.

"Jenna and Matt are last," Abbi whispered. "Wouldn't you know!"

"They'll have to be great to beat that last pair." Dan shook his head.

A hush fell over the auditorium as the music began for Jenna and Matt's dance. The lights were low and the stage almost dark. Jenna came from the wings on one side, Matt from the other.

Lauren''s eyes were fixed on Matt.

On the darkened stage, Jenna watched Matt approach from the opposite wing, waiting for the music cue. When the dance started she led him through the first series of steps they had created. This was so different from her dream of a glittering ballet stage! She and Matt danced as equals. Instead of a helpless, fluttering swan, she was a partner as they struggled together to find a way out of their prison.

The shaking and bad nerves were gone. This kind of dancing meant thinking about your partner and forgetting yourself. There was no room for worrying about being perfect. Jenna felt powerful and free.

In the audience, Abbi was squeezing Lauren's

hand, whispering, "Aren't they beautiful!" over and over.

"Oh, Lauren, you're crying," Abbi said, when the dance ended. She handed Lauren a tissue from her pocket. "I don't blame you," she sniffed. "Wasn't it brilliant?"

"If they don't win," Dan muttered, "the judges are out to lunch." Dan and Abbi surged up on the stage with half the other kids in the audience to congratulate their friends.

Lauren got up from her plush seat. She pushed her way to the edge of the aisle. She looked up at the lighted stage, crowded with well-wishers, waiting for the judges' decision. She could see Matt and Jenna, surrounded by their friends.

She wouldn't wait. She would go for what she wanted – now!

☆

Jenna's mother threw her arms around her. Joyce hugged them both. "I just can't believe what I saw up there!" Her mother was shaking her head. "I kept saying, 'Is that my Jenna, so beautiful, so talented?' Your dad would have been so proud!"

"I take back everything I ever said about dancing being a waste of time," Joyce said. "You were great, kid."

Jenna bent down so she could rest her head on her mother's shoulder. She didn't need words. Out of the corner of her eye she saw Lauren talking to Matt. He was leaning down so he could hear her above the laughter and congratulations.

☆ CHAPTER TWENTY ☆

Questions and Answers

"Matt, I have something I have to tell you!" Lauren shouted. "I know it's a funny time to be saying it, but please listen!"

"I'm listening." Matt put his hand on Lauren's shoulder.

"I...I think you're amazing," Lauren began.

"Oh..." Matt's worried face lit with relief and happiness. "Is that all? Thanks, Lauren. I just hope for Jenna's sake we win, but it felt good anyway."

"No, I don't mean your dancing. I'm trying to tell you..." Lauren straightened her shoulders. "I'm trying to tell you that I like you very much, and I have ever since the first day I saw you at auditions. And I want to know how you feel about me."

The worried frown came back to Matt's face. He pulled Lauren to one side, near the curtains. "I...this is hard to say, Lauren, because I think you're wonderful, but I...we're too young, at least I'm too young. I want us all to be friends, that's all..."

"But maybe, in the future?" Lauren looked seriously into his brown eyes. There was no laughter there now.

Matt shook his head. "Who knows? But I don't think so, Lauren." He looked over his shoulder to where Jenna was standing with her mother and sister. "But don't feel bad. I know how you feel. It's kind of always been Jenna, for me. I mean, that's why I came to Holly in the first place…"

Lauren gulped. "It is?"

Matt turned away. "Here comes my family," he laughed shakily. "Prepare for a tidal wave. Stay, Lauren. I feel like you're one of my sisters."

But Lauren slipped into the wings, the tears sliding helplessly down her cheeks. She didn't want to be Matt's sister.

☆

The dancers and their audience were back in their seats. A hush fell over the auditorium as Mary Adaman stepped gracefully to centre stage with an envelope in one hand, and a gold trophy in the other.

"Here it comes!" Matt squeezed Jenna's hand in the darkness.

"I wish our sponsors had provided scholarships for all our students," Miss Adaman said, "because I am very proud of all of our dancers tonight, and I know how hard all of them worked. Unfortunately, there is only one scholarship and one place at the New York City Dance Impression Workshop next spring. I am pleased to announce that this years winners are…" she paused, "Jenna James and Matt Caruso!"

To thundering applause, Jenna and Matt

squirmed out of their seats and ran up onto the stage.

☆

An hour later, Jenna was clutching the dance trophy to her heart while Matt waved the envelope aloft to the loud cheers of his friends in the canteen.

"We did it," he beamed at Jenna. "I always knew we would. New York, here we come!"

"Did your parents really say you could go?" Jenna asked.

"My dad would rather I was a football player," Matt laughed, "but he won't stop me. And Ma is thrilled. She thinks I'll be another 'Lord of the Dance'. Matt did a little Irish jig of pure joy.

"And with this," Jenna set the shiny trophy on their usual table, "my mum and sister will stop suggesting I go to modelling school for the summer, and learn the catwalk walk."

"Look out, here comes Abbi," Matt laughed. "We're about to get swept away by another tidal wave."

Abbi, hair flying, grabbed Jenna by both hands and swung her around. "You won! Oh, I'm so happy!" The joy radiated out of Abbi's face like a solar flare.

Dan clapped Matt on the back. "You were terrific," he grinned. "If I was writing a review, I'd say that Matt Caruso and Jennifer James took dancing to new heights today."

"Is that some kind of lame joke about my height?" Jenna laughed.

"Let's just say there's no ceiling on your talent," Dan grinned. It was clear he was as pleased as anyone by their success.

"Where's Lauren?" Abbi asked suddenly. "She was sitting with us during the competition. She was crying her eyes out when you guys were dancing."

Jenna felt a stab of guilt. Lauren! Where was she and what was she feeling? I need to talk to her, Jenna thought.

Matt was quiet. "She's somewhere around…" he muttered. He and Jenna exchanged quick glances.

Lauren was propelling her way towards their table. There was a flush of excitement high on each cheek and a determined look in her eye.

There's something different about her, Jenna thought, half alarmed. What's happened?

"Congratulations!" Lauren reached up and kissed Jenna on the cheek. "You two were absolutely great!"

"Where did you disappear to?" Abbi asked. "I turned round and you were gone."

"I just called the Lilith Singers," Lauren said. "I told them I'd love to tour with them this Christmas."

"That's wonderful!"

"Way to go, Lauren!"

Congratulations showered around Lauren. Jenna breathed a sigh of relief.

"William said they have a big grant to hire more performers," Lauren wasn't finished with her good news. "If any of you want a job over the holidays…"

Dan jumped up. "Dan the juggling man, at their service!" he cried. "Lauren, you're a genius. Give me that number – I'm going to call before they get someone else. Abbi? Are you interested?"

"I'd love to, but I can't. I have to go to Australia–" Abbi started to say, shaking her head. Suddenly she stopped. Emotions crossed her face like spring storms – first clouds of doubt, then thunderbolts of inspiration.

"YES!" she screamed "YES, I'LL DO IT!"

"But what about Christmas in Australia?" Jenna asked.

"Don't you see?" Abbi grabbed her excitedly. "Joe should go to Australia by himself! There isn't enough money for both of us, anyway. And this way he and Dad can start a whole new father-son relationship, and I won't have to baby-sit, and I can join the group and–"

"And look exactly like you stepped out of a medieval portrait to play the tambourine," Dan finished.

"But what about those beaches?" Matt laughed. "And the kangaroos?"

"They'll still be hopping next year," Abbi waved her hands. "Come on, Dan, let's go and phone."

They dashed off together, cutting a swathe through the crowd. Matt's family appeared and crowded around him, leading him away. Suddenly, Jenna and Lauren were alone together. They looked at each other across the table.

"I guess you can't join the Lillith Singers," Lauren said. "You and Matt will be practising for New York."

"Lauren, I have something to tell you–" Jenna started.

"Don't worry," Lauren shook her head. "I straightened everything out with Matt. He…he doesn't…I don't know if I can stop caring about him, but at least I know he doesn't feel that way about me."

Jenna looked down. "I'm sorry," she said.

"Don't be." Lauren reached for her hand. "Matt's right. We're too young to have serious feelings about each other, anyway." Lauren's small face managed a real grin. "And who knows what will happen in the future, right? I guess I have to try folk singing and see if it's my thing."

The clouds cleared from Jenna's face. Lauren was right. You never did know what was going to happen in the future. She felt a glow of happiness. All of her dreams were coming true. Not the way she planned, but somehow even better. You had to let dreams unfold, she thought, you couldn't plan or control how things happened.

"You know what a terrible singer I am," she told Lauren, "but I'd love to work backstage for your group at Christmas. It will be fun!"

Preview the next

STAGE SCHOOL

NOW...

Lauren – Drastic Decisions

☆CHAPTER ONE☆

Crying in the Night

Lauren woke up to the sound of someone crying. At first, she thought she must be dreaming. There were no small children in her house, and it was the middle of the night. Lauren checked the square of darkness outside her window, then rolled over to look at the clock. 3:09 said the red letters. But someone was crying, downstairs!

Lauren climbed out of her warm bed, felt her way to the light switch on the wall, and found her dressing gown hanging on the cupboard door. She paused before stepping out into the hall.

The crying sounds were softer now – no longer wails, but sobs. Lauren tiptoed down the wide curved stairs of her house. A crack of light showed under the music room doors. The sobbing seemed to be coming from in there.

"Hello?" Lauren tapped on the sliding wooden doors.

There was a moment of breathless silence and

Lauren tapped again. "Is someone in there?"

She slid open the doors. A baby grand piano stood in one corner of the room. In the dim light of the lamp over the piano's music rack, she could see her mother's bent head. Her dark hair hid her face.

"Mum?" Lauren tucked her own fair hair behind her ears and took a nervous step forward. She felt as if she was trespassing on a private moment. She had never seen her mother cry.

"I'm sorry I woke you." Her mother's voice was muffled. Her face was buried in a large photo album.

Lauren wished she had stayed in bed. "That's OK," she said. "What's wrong?"

Her mother swivelled round on the piano stool, clutching the album to her chest.

Lauren gave a gasp as she recognized it. It was her music scrapbook! Her mother had been going through all her old newspaper clippings All those ancient pictures of her in frilly dresses winning prizes at music festivals!

"How can you ask what's wrong?" Her mother's face was in shadow, but her voice was full of blame. "Your singing teacher called today. She wants to stop your lessons."

Lauren felt a stab of guilt and anger. She'd been studying with Mrs Bainbridge since she was six years old. At her last lesson she had been furious with Lauren for not memorizing her practice piece. But how dare she call and say that to her mother!

"She says you're just wasting her time with this

folk music you want to sing. Oh, Lauren! What's happened? You could do anything you wanted with a voice like yours – right to the top in opera, if you wanted – and you're wasting it on that pitiful performing arts school!"

"It's not pitiful!" Lauren felt her anger rise. Ever since she'd been accepted at the William S. Holly Stage School, she'd been having this battle with her parents.

"It's those friends of yours!" Her mother shook her head. "They're just not the kind of people you should be associating with! They're the ones who are turning you away from serious music."

"That's not true!" Lauren cried. She thought of her friends – the tall, beautiful Jenna, passionately devoted to dance, Abbi with her flying gold-blonde hair, and her burning desire to be a star, and Dan, with his funny, kind ways. And then there was Matt.

Matt Caruso's face had been in Lauren's mind from the moment she had met him at last summer's Stage School auditions. It didn't matter that he treated her like a little sister. It was really because of Matt that she was at William S. Holly, though she wouldn't admit that to anyone!

"I don't want to sing opera – why can't you understand?" Lauren pleaded. "Stage School is where my friends are, and where I want to be." But even as she said it, Lauren felt a pang. In the last few weeks, things hadn't been going well for her at William S. Holly.

But her mother's idea of an alternative was to

go back to the very proper girls' school where she had been studying, and to spend every spare hour practising operatic arias!

She had no burning wish to perform, to sing opera in front of crowds of people. That's what her parents wanted – what they'd been training her for and pushing her towards since she was six.

"A talent like yours…"Lauren could hear the tears in her mother's voice again. "It's a gift. People dream of being able to sing like that, and you just want to throw it all away."

Lauren could hear footsteps on the stairs behind her. It must be her father, coming to see what was wrong.

"Let's go to bed, Mum," Lauren pleaded. She dreaded getting into this conversation with her dad, especially in the middle of the night!

"You go ahead," her mother sighed. Lauren slipped past her into the kitchen, and made her way to her room up the back stairs. She climbed into bed and clenched the covers under her chin, listening to the raised voices of her parents below.

"I just can't watch her throw her life away like this!" she heard her mother moan.

"Well, it does no good to stay up all night," her father was saying. "You'll just make yourself ill."

Lauren clenched the covers tighter. How much more of this could she stand? It was as if she'd left home and become a drug addict at thirteen, the way they talked about her!

☆

The next morning, Lauren's father was alone in the

kitchen fixing a breakfast tray, when she went down. He turned to look at her.

"Your mother's not well," he said. "She didn't sleep much last night."

"What's wrong?" Lauren asked, knowing what a stupid question it was. She was what was wrong, the cause of all the problems in their family.

"She's anxious about you," Lauren's father looked tired, too. "The news about your singing lessons came as a shock. She thought…we both thought you might get over this Stage School thing." He looked down.

Lauren felt her heart wrench. She and her dad had always been close. Now, he barely spoke to her, and when he did it was in this cold, flat voice.

"If you could just understand…" Lauren started.

"I know…your friends," her father sighed. "I'm afraid your friends are leading you down the wrong path – away from the music you love and your real future. I'm afraid I do understand."

He always cut off conversations that way, Lauren thought furiously, as she watched her father carry her mother's breakfast tray out of the room. Why couldn't she talk to him – tell him how she felt? She wanted to call after him, but the words just stuck in her throat.

Torn between two worlds – will Lauren do what her parents want, or will she follow her heart? Read on in…

Stage School 4
☆Lauren – Drastic Decisions☆

Have you read the other Stage School stories?